T0030929

THE
DAYS
OF
AFREKETE

THE
DAYS
OF
AFREKETE

◎◎◎

Asali Solomon

FARRAR, STRAUS AND GIROUX   NEW YORK

Farrar, Straus and Giroux
120 Broadway, New York 10271

Library of Congress Cataloging-in-Publication Data
Names: Solomon, Asali, author.
Title: The days of Afrekete / Asali Solomon.
Description: First edition. | New York : Farrar, Straus and Giroux, 2021.
Identifiers: LCCN 2021021361 | ISBN 9780374140052 (hardcover)
Classification: LCC PS3619.O4335 D39 2021 | DDC 813/.6—dc23
LC record available at https://lccn.loc.gov/2021021361

Designed by Abby Kagan

Our books may be purchased in bulk for promotional, educational, or business use.
Please contact your local bookseller or the Macmillan Corporate and
Premium Sales Department at 1-800-221-7945, extension 5442, or by email at
MacmillanSpecialMarkets@macmillan.com.

www.fsgbooks.com
www.twitter.com/fsgbooks • www.facebook.com/fsgbooks

1 3 5 7 9 10 8 6 4 2

For the Solomons and the Friedmans
and for every Black woman
everywhere

Don't let me be lonely . . .

PAUL CELAN

JAMES TAYLOR

THE ISLEY BROTHERS

CLAUDIA RANKINE

THE
DAYS
OF
AFREKETE

1

L ate one April afternoon, Liselle stood at the large kitchen window rubbing her hands together for warmth. Gripping the phone to her ear with her shoulder, she acknowledged that early spring was her least favorite time of year. Letting the idea settle, she felt herself slide down into one of the chairs at the cluttered kitchen island. She had intended to stand and take this call, keep a straight spine and spacious diaphragm, but found she could not.

"Jail, Liselle. They're gonna put his ass in jail."

"But, Ma," she said, half expecting to see a cloud of steam come out of her mouth. It was not cold enough for the heat to kick on, and yet the air inside her 150-year-old home in Northwest Philadelphia felt icy. "Just because the FBI said something doesn't mean it's true. What about Martin Luther . . ."

Verity let out an acid whoop of laughter. "You sound insane. Do I need to say that Winn is not Martin Luther King? Shit, these days, Winn up here looking more like J. Edgar—"

"Not funny," snapped Liselle. She did feel an urge to laugh, but as if she were being tickled by someone bigger who did not love her. She imagined herself in the future, taking a panicked call from her son, Patrice, and resolved to do better than Verity was doing to comfort her, even as she suspected she would fail.

"We don't even know if he did anything," Liselle insisted. "Yes, this guy told me they're going to indict him—but we don't know what he did, or even *what they say* he did."

The daylight was gray and the dark wood fixtures in the house weighed her down. She felt a gentle tugging, which, if she gave into it, would take her briefly out of her body. Her mother's voice snapped her back.

"Liselle, are you listening to yourself?"

"Ma, look, I . . . I just want to know if you think I should cancel this dinner party."

"Well, I'm not sure what's being celebrated. Is it Winn losing the primary—which we always knew he would? Church Williams has held that office so long that you were bucktoothed and *skinny* when they swore him in."

"Look, the party is to thank the folks who helped us." Liselle felt sheepish at her use of "folks." She had no memory of saying the word before Winn decided to run for office.

"Oh, the *folks*," Verity said, on cue. "Did you invite the *folks* who are gonna get him locked up? Because somebody was talking to somebody, right?"

Liselle hadn't even considered that she and Winn were potentially about to host an FBI informant. Would that person really have had the gall to accept their invitation?

"To the point," Verity said. "You want to know if you should throw a party to thank these people who had nothing better to do with their money and time than to help you delude yourselves?"

"It wasn't a delusion," said Liselle, her cheeks warming. She had used the exact same word, "delusion," in an argument with Winn early in the campaign, when there had been time to turn back, when she was trying to make him turn back. She was surprised and irritated to find herself defending his—and her—honor. But she persisted, as she often found herself doing when her mother goaded her. "Look, Ma, at one point in the polls—"

Verity laughed. "The polls! Where did he buy those polls? I hope he kept the receipts!"

"Look, can't you just fucking say if you think I should cancel the party?"

Verity began to breathe.

Since she'd been "on sabbatical" from teaching (an unpaid leave, really), Liselle had taken yoga classes with a frequency that shamed her. She regularly tried out different studios in Mt. Airy and Chestnut Hill during the city's most productive hours. In her only neighborhood celebrity sighting of Sonia Sanchez, Liselle could not greet her, so galled had she been to be wearing spandex and clutching a BPA-free water bottle with a mat under her arm. But she had learned enough from the classes that listening to Verity's loud exhalations reminded her of the practice of *ujjayi*: "triumphantly victorious breath."

Liselle's forty-one years of research suggested that no matter how distant, abusive, judgmental, unloving, and useless one's mother was, one called her when things fell apart. One called one's mother and told her things no one else knew, even if all she said in response was *It is what it is/All I can do is pray for you/Just be glad you have a roof over your head/I told you so, but you wouldn't listen/Oh, please, he was always like that. You made your choice/You know my money is tied up in this house right now.* For weeks, since she'd spoken to the attractive gentleman from the FBI in the coffee shop, Liselle had wanted desperately *not* to call Verity.

Of course, part of the reason she hadn't was that she hadn't even been properly alarmed. It felt almost inconceivable to Liselle that Winn's political ambition, so sudden and half-hearted, had led him into anything illegal. And yet she had not had the nerve to ask him the truth about what was going on, nor told him what she had heard from the FBI man.

"Liselle"—oh, the singular sound of one's mother saying one's name—"I don't know why you're suddenly so interested in my opinion. I haven't seen you do a single thing I've suggested since you were seven. As long as Patrice—my poor Patrice—is okay, I don't care what happens over there. It does not matter if you cancel this *fucking* dinner party, but maybe you could go back in time and cancel this godforsaken campaign, which was a huge waste of time, money, and tears. Then, after you look into that, you can go ahead and cancel this marriage too."

Liselle hung up the phone and listened to her heart slamming away in her chest.

A thought reached out and grabbed her. With the same reckless spirit with which she'd hung up on her mother, she dialed another number she was shocked to find she remembered. "Is Selena there?" Then she left her name, number, and a one-word message, hanging up before the person who'd answered the phone could ask her about it.

2

Liselle had met the agent twice before his call. He'd been at one of Winn's campaign rallies, though she hadn't known who he was at the time. Later she'd run into him at the Chestnut Hill Café. She bristled with hatred, remembering his dopey name and the fact that he was a tall and extremely good-looking Black man. All of this had caught her off guard from the beginning. The next thing she knew he was calling the house "as a courtesy," he said, to warn her that the FBI was pursuing indictments against Winn.

Liselle went over all of it again and again in her mind, while keeping her body in motion. She shuffled the piles of nonsense, making room for the catering delivery. She stacked envelopes and flyers, an expensive traffic ticket she hoped someone had paid online, an outtake from the family photo session they'd sat for in the early days of the campaign. The photo shoot had captured exactly what it was—the aftermath of a three-hour argument about the state of Patrice's hair. She rewiped the spotless counter; it kept her from falling through the floor.

"When will all of this happen?" she'd asked the FBI man.

"Soon," he'd said.

"I just don't understand. You said he hadn't done anything."

"I know I didn't say that." He'd chuckled gently, sounding like a *Quiet Storm* DJ.

Liselle checked her watch, an unadorned black waterproof model with a silicone band. Winn had once tried to replace it, gifting her a platinum one that cost more than her mother's monthly salary from the city Department of Licenses and Inspections. When he'd lost the primary, Liselle had quietly placed it back in its velvet box in her underwear drawer. Maybe she could sell it. Further, she wondered if you could collect life insurance on a spouse if they went to prison. Of course, she would go back to work as had always been planned, but could she and Patrice survive the genteel poverty of one private school teaching salary?

Less than four hours remained before the party; Winn would likely arrive not long before the guests. Before that Patrice would be home from school and Liselle had to plan what she would say, what she would do, how her face would look. ("Fix your face, Liselle," Verity had often said when she was young.)

Years ago, when she and Winn had first started having people to dinner, Liselle had despised it. First there was the matter of having nothing to talk about with the menacingly dull lawyers at Winn's firm. Then there was the fact that even as he rarely lifted a finger toward the execution, Winn micromanaged the plans. Even when Liselle was working full-time and took on the bulk of the management of Patrice, Winn felt perfectly comfortable turning up his nose at menu ideas, or insisting on the unused decorative plates only found in restaurants ("chargers," they were called).

Along the way, as the years passed and Winn made partner, Liselle had become what guests described as "a gracious hostess." She winced inwardly each time at the female weakness of the description, as well as at the pressure to keep up the act. And after every party she greeted the departure of the last guest with the triumphant sense of having come down alive from a small mountain. It would not be so tonight, she thought, when the end of the party might also be the end of everything else. Liselle toyed with an image of herself and Patrice moving boxes into her mother's cluttered, dark house in West Philadelphia.

To think she had spent the day shopping for cheese and flowers—had gone to shops at either end of Germantown Avenue looking in vain for calla lilies. This was not like the movies, where things worked out for you because you were a sympathetic character. Experience did not bear out the religion that so many people clung to: "God doesn't give you more than you can handle." Of course, God did that to people every single minute of every single day.

"This doesn't feel real," she had said to William McMichael on the phone. It was happening so fast, fast like the night they went to bed and there was a stupid old white president and when they awoke there was a smart, youngish Black one, such an unprecedented state of affairs that barely a decade before that there had been a bumper crop of shows and movies about the inherently comic situation of a Black president.

Liselle was no longer moving but standing still, limbs filled with sand, giving a respectful audience to these thoughts. She jumped when the doorbell rang. "Soon," William McMichael had said.

As she walked toward the front door, terror at the back of her throat, she remembered hopefully that Jimena, her helper, was coming to prepare for the party. But the figure on the porch was neither Jimena nor the FBI.

"Hello, Mrs. Anderson," said Xochitl, Jimena's daughter. "My mom's knees were bothering her. Sorry I had to ring the bell; we don't have a key anymore." Unspoken: Jimena used to have a key, but after Winn announced his bid for office, he had made a paranoid argument for changing the locks and not giving a new key to Jimena. Or to Verity, for that matter. (Liselle had overruled him on the issue of Verity.)

"That's okay. I hope Jim—your mom is okay," Liselle said. Unspoken: Xochitl's name, which Liselle seemed to mispronounce each time she said it, as well as Jimena's, which Liselle was also shy of pronouncing.

"She's fine," said Xochitl. "She's just getting older, you know, so I help her out when I have time in my schedule." Unspoken: Liselle had an old woman with bad knees scrubbing her toilets and loading her dishwasher; also unspoken: Xochitl, a PhD student and immigration rights activist, was lowering herself to work for Liselle, who had never finished, nor started, a master's degree. "She may come by later if she's feeling up to it."

"Oh, nice," said Liselle, pasting a smile on her face. Jimena and Xochitl working together always divided Liselle's feelings. When she heard snatches of their gentle Spanish after a glass or two of wine at her dinner parties, Liselle sometimes entertained the thought that she was helping mother and daughter spend quality time together. On the other hand, she had no idea what they were saying and wondered if they were talking about her. She felt her ever twoness as the Black mistress of a tiny plantation.

"So, what do we have today?" Xochitl asked, returning the stiff smile. Even a fake smile (Liselle knew because she'd seen the real one) lit up Xochitl's face. Liselle wondered if that was the kind of thing a slave mistress would notice—the lovely smiles of her slaves?

Liselle walked Xochitl into the kitchen and showed her boxes of frozen mushroom tarts, blocks of Gouda, the wheel of Brie, and gestured toward the serving dishes. Years ago, at a law firm dinner party, Liselle had picked up the frugal trick of providing one's own Costco appetizers. No one much cared about the crackers at these things.

"The caterers will be here soon; you should listen for the doorbell."

Xochitl looked up from the kitchen island, which Liselle had not completely cleared, though she'd arranged the trash into admirable piles. "Are you going out?" she asked.

"No," Liselle said with the air of an apology.

"Anything else, Mrs. Anderson?"

"Please call me Liselle. Anderson is my husband's name." Liselle tried to soften the edge of her voice. "Or Ms. Belmont, if that's more comfortable."

"I apologize," said Xochitl, shifting from one foot to another. "I hope I haven't done or said anything to offend you. My mother really needs this job."

"Of course. She'll have it as long as she wants." As she said it, Liselle realized this was less true today than it had been yesterday. They would not need household help if Winn was arrested and they became social outcasts of an uncertain financial future.

Many years ago, Jimena, whose husband had been repeatedly deported back to Puebla—the third time for good—had asked for help to pay for knee replacement surgery and Xochitl's Catholic school tuition. The people who knew about these things had told Liselle that you did not get involved with housekeeping staff on that level. It could open the door to a continuous stream of requests and a tightening entanglement of dependence. Though Liselle had blamed Winn in her apologetic refusal, he had actually shrugged at the five-figure amount Jimena had requested. It had been Liselle who'd denied her.

Jimena had finally managed to get the surgery, but maybe too late. She walked with a limp. Xochitl had briefly had to transfer to a public school, where some girls had tried to set her long hair on fire, before she was rescued by a scholarship. Liselle was thinking that maybe if she had been more generous, the universe would not be bearing down on her family as it was.

"You didn't offend me," said Liselle. She imagined herself making a pot of tea, sitting down with Xochitl to tell her everything that was happening. It would begin when Winn had said, over an anniversary dinner nearly two years ago, "So, some people approached me about getting into politics," and end with her fear that the FBI would barge in during her party. She pictured Xochitl's compassionate and wise expression.

. . . , she would say, reaching for Liselle's hand.

"I'm going to get to work then, Mrs., uh, Belmont," said the actual Xochitl.

"Oh, of course," said Liselle. As she headed upstairs to change her clothes and hide, she heard humming. Maybe Xochitl knew everything that was happening. Maybe she had set them up. Liselle could not decide which one—the fantasy that Xochitl would comfort her, or the fantasy of betrayal—made her feel more like she was wearing a hoopskirt and waving her lace fan at Xochitl, across a gulf, from the wrong side of history.

3

She knew it was a mistake to hug Patrice, but she couldn't stop herself. At the sound of his feet on the stairs, she was in the hallway; once her arms were around him, she found it difficult to let go. Squeezing, she breathed in his sweaty-socks-and-oatmeal smell.

He wriggled and pushed her away, first gently, then with some firmness. "What are you doing? Dad here?"

"Does Dad usually come home before dark?" She laughed harshly. "It's Xochitl."

"*Xochitl,*" said Patrice, pronouncing the name slowly and looking (down) at her.

Liselle ignored the correction. "So, you're going to Adam's house tonight." Earlier she had arranged this with Miriam Blau, who lived a few blocks away. Patrice and her son had once legitimately been friends, and now they were forced-family-friends, even as the families were barely convivial at this point. It was enough for Liselle for tonight.

Patrice wiggled his nose in distaste. "Nah, I'm good. I'm just going to go hit this homework, then put on a clean shirt and come eat fig chicken with the phonies."

"Nope," said Liselle. "This is too complicated tonight. You can go do your homework and play video games with Adam."

"You know Adam does drugs," Patrice said solemnly, one eye twitching. It was all Liselle could do not to laugh in his face. She thought of a conversation she'd had with Winn a few months prior; they'd collapsed merrily with laughter, agreeing that Patrice was a terrible liar. "How does he even get his one eye to do that?" Liselle had asked Winn. "He could never," Winn said, gasping for breath, "go into politics."

"Please just drop it, sweetheart. I'm sorry to uninvite you to a party in your own house, but Dad losing the election is not a very fun reason for a party anyway, right?"

Patrice muttered to himself, reminding Liselle of Verity. Then, as Verity sometimes did, he became abruptly loud. "You said Miriam was a 'second-wave hypocrite menace.' Remember that?"

"Lower your voice," murmured Liselle, glancing nervously in the direction of the back stairs, which led to the kitchen. She couldn't bear the thought of Xochitl imagining her as an incompetent New Age parent (on top of not being able to take care of her own house, and being married to a white man). As for Patrice, Liselle thought if he kept pushing, she might lose it and tell him everything that was going on. But then maybe he wouldn't be surprised that Winn had cut corners in his bid for office; he had certainly done so in his parenting. Four years ago, in a bizarre sequence of events, Liselle had gone to Boston for a teachers' conference and came back to find that Winn had been burrowed away in his office downtown and had left nine-year-old Patrice at Ms. Lumley's next door, where he had eaten stale Italian waffle cookies for dinner and spent most of the night on a pee-smelling couch.

Liselle took a deep breath. "Patrice. My problems with Miriam are not your business. I need you to head over there right now."

"*Fine!*" yelled Patrice. Briefly, and not for the first time, Liselle imagined strangling him. As if intuiting this, he then spoke in a normal voice. "You win. I'll go take unmarked pills at Adam's house and *not* listen to Miriam talk about how '08 was 'Hillary's turn.'" He used his fingers to make scare quotes. Taking the stairs two at a time, he headed down and out of the house, trying his hardest to slam the heavy front door.

Liselle stood for an instant in the empty hallway and then entered her own room, closing the door quietly to show everyone (Xochitl, downstairs) that civility and restraint had returned. Then, though she had just taken the trouble to put on a crisp white shirt, she collapsed on her unmade bed. Her body surged with the anticipation of future scenes, uglier and even more shameful.

4

After Patrice was gone and the house felt resettled, Liselle jumped once again at the sound of the doorbell. She sat straight up and listened to Xochitl walking toward the door, exhaling only when she heard the familiar voices of the caterers. A few minutes later she heard Winn call out, "Home again, home again, lickety-split."

He had to say that when he entered the house. Years ago, before they'd met, Winn had had occasional bouts of OCD, which he'd described to her (strategically?) after their wedding invites had been sent. Fortunately, it had dwindled to reciting this refrain whenever he walked in the door. Even under the stress of the election, he confined himself to "lickety-split," which was much milder than what he had taken up in college—when he'd intoned a Christina Rossetti poem about death as he washed his hands for twenty-five minutes. With a swampy feeling in her gut, Liselle tried to imagine rituals he might obsessively perform in prison.

She had not wanted Winn to get involved in politics. Their life together had been comfortable, with moments of joy. It was true that for her, frankly, those moments had grown muted and dependent on trifles: the alcohol content of a fussy cocktail, the distance between the beach and the condo in Lewes, which had seemed so short back when they'd first bought the place. Still, she had known that her life with Winn and Patrice was good, enviable even. It would have seemed to child-Liselle like a distant dream back when she was growing up with an exhausted Verity, in a house that sometimes smelled of roach spray. She had escaped that house and a life like her mother's, that is, until she was on the phone with her mother, who said, "Jail."

Or perhaps her escape had ended when Winn first told her about the people who'd approached him about running for Congress. She had not challenged him when he spoke about his desire to "get involved." She had not pointed out the obvious, which was that he lacked vision and passion, and that he was simply bored and wanting to feel special. Liselle knew there was a hole in him, and he had kept throwing things into it: first Liselle, then Patrice, then making partner at the firm. She had not pressed him, because, in fact, Winn's campaign and the fantasy of his victory had become what she threw into the widening hole inside of *her*.

At the beginning of the campaign discussions, she'd seen fleeting images of herself as a different person, with a higher sheen (though not on her nose); she would shrink back down to a size eight or even smaller, but her jewelry would gain weight. In these sequences, Herself wore color-blocked suits and had a neat permed bob, instead of a natural cropped close every two weeks to camouflage her thinning hairline. She and Winn stood at a podium raising the clasped hands of victory. It could happen to anyone; if a Black man with a name that Verity had initially mocked could be president of the United States, surely Liselle could be the wife of a lousy state representative. In fact, early on they had talked about Liselle at a strategy session, potentially as part of the formula for unseating Church Williams, who'd been in office "since the book of Judges."

The muffled sound of Winn greeting Xochitl (Liselle thought

with shame of the girl hearing him say "lickety-split") was drowned out by the ringing phone on her bedside table.

"I'm coming home," said Patrice.

"Patrice," Liselle said with a heavy sigh, "have you ever needed me, like, really needed me to do anything for you?"

"Come on, Mom. Don't do that."

"Well, let's think for a minute, but just a minute, because I have a *shit*load of things to do, a *fuck*load of things," Liselle continued, though this was, strictly speaking, a lie, and she knew that Patrice felt uncomfortable when she cursed. She knew exactly how he felt—the way she herself had felt as she watched her mother drink beer, getting blurrier and blurrier. Liselle had learned to put herself to bed at the age of six.

"Do you remember the time in second grade when you—"

"Fine!" Patrice slammed down the phone. Liselle knew it was wrong of her to allude to the time he was eight and soiled his shorts, and she'd had to race across town to pick him up from day camp, clean up the administrator's office, and spend the rest of the summer amusing him instead of studying for her GREs.

"What was that about?" Winn asked. "Also are you lying in *bed*?" Suddenly her husband was in the room, eating a lollipop. He did it to keep from smoking, but it sometimes made Liselle want to smack him. It also made her want lollipops, and she sometimes found herself sucking one with no memory of having gone into the ceramic jar in the kitchen where they were kept.

She arched one eyebrow at him. "Are you eating candy?"

"I asked my questions first." Winn's eyes twinkled and he pushed back a lock of hair. He had the look of someone who had aged out of playing the rich jerk in an eighties teen movie. "Liselle, it wasn't a criticism. It seems like a good idea, being in bed. Whose idea was this party anyway?"

Liselle grunted as he reclined beside her and hoisted himself up on one arm.

"Shoes," Liselle said. She was annoyed to hear Verity's voice coming out of her mouth, but sometimes Verity said what needed to be said.

"Who was on the phone?" Winn asked, untying his laces.

"I sent Patrice to Miriam Blau's house. He was trying to come back home."

Winn sucked contemplatively. "I kind of thought he might like to be here tonight. You don't think it's a good idea for all of us to get some closure on this?"

Liselle studied him. She wasn't sure when, but she knew it was definitely before the campaign that she had begun wondering whether what had drawn them together was no longer there. Maybe it had never been there. Their union had been a lark, a not-quite-bohemian adventure. But then one day Winn was campaigning for public office and now he was saying "closure." These were the things earnest people, earnestly married, did.

"I really think," Winn continued, removing his lollipop for emphasis, "that you're going about this all wrong, babe."

"That might be true. But I didn't feel like having him underfoot while these people—"

"Our friends—"

"—*your* friends, pick over your political carcass. Too many different emotional weather systems."

"That is a *lot* of figurative language. Like a pileup of metaphors. Shit, I just added to it. By the way, I invited Ron Mack tonight. I noticed he wasn't on the list."

"Do you think we still need him around?" Liselle asked, the swampy feeling returning. Whatever bad things were happening to them, she suspected Ron was involved.

"Look," Winn said, "I know you hate the guy's guts, but he really did a lot for me."

"I think it's safe to say he was looking for something in return."

"'I think it's safe to say he was looking for something in return,'" Winn repeated in a high, nagging voice. "My goodness, maybe you should save some of this witty repartee for the party. By all means, engage in a gentle war of words with Ron Mack. All I ask is that you display your thinnest veneer of civility. I don't even mind seeing the cracks."

Liselle snorted, trying not to laugh. "Whatever you want. But I'm leaving Patrice where he is."

With a languid motion, Winn tossed his lollipop stick toward the wastebasket. It hit the lip and landed on the floor. "Layup," he said. Then he fell back in the same shape as Liselle, arms tight at his sides. "Now we can play vampire together." He reached for her hand and she let him take it. *Tell him about the call, the FBI. Ask him what he did. Now.* Thinking but not speaking, she squeezed then dropped his hand and went to set up her computer so a playlist called "Dinner with Edge" would play for almost four hours on the system that piped through the house.

"Ex-Factor" bloomed from the house speaker, Lauryn Hill in the fullest voice she'd ever have. She thought of a photo of Lauryn Hill in a yellow dress, her lips the color of red velvet cake. There had been a time, after college, when Liselle had regularly searched Lauryn Hill out on the internet, looking for a sign that she would turn it around. Instead she encountered pictures of her looking washed-out, wearing a Christian cult member getup. Her hair looked abruptly cut, reminding Liselle of little African girls who, between walking miles to school, dealing with tamponless menstruation, and carrying water for their families, didn't have time for Western beauty standards. Liselle read that the press was forced to refer to her as "Ms. Lauryn Hill" and that she had five children by her beautiful husband, rumored to be a philanderer. Liselle had stopped searching her out on the internet, but she sometimes thought she'd give much of what she had to find out exactly what had happened to Lauryn Hill.

These days, the image of Lauryn Hill came into Liselle's mind when she thought of Selena Octave. As she listened to the song (*care for me, care for me*), she wondered if Selena had gotten her message.

5

They'd met twenty years before the Mt. Airy dinner party, on the first day of Liselle's final year and the first day of Selena's first year at Bryn Mawr College. At that time, though she was only twenty-one, Liselle had felt worn-out and heavy with a sense of the end. After nearly four years, Liselle had found a place for herself behind the gates, among the stone buildings and elegant archways, all of which had once seemed an alien planet. She was one of the top students in the Anthropology Department, invited to be a student representative on a search committee; she had a rapport with the department administrator, an older Puerto Rican woman who fed her muffins meant for faculty gatherings. Of course, Liselle had always been a teacher's pet. What was (had been?) miraculous at Bryn Mawr was the position she'd achieved among the students.

In 1994, Liselle walked the campus grounds, reflecting on her trajectory. She remembered keenly showing up to college in a leather motorcycle jacket she'd saved to buy. Though it was clearly too warm for animal hide, she'd worn it with her permed hair pulled tightly back into a ponytail, paired with huge hoop earrings à la Sade. She was not, at that time, a lesbian, but a socially awkward virgin, who had spent high school pining for wildly unattainable boys, the basketball star who was also a science fair champion and the talented weed-dealing DJ, a tall reddish-colored boy so attractive that teachers leered. Later Liselle knew she had chosen those particular boys to stave off the possibility of dating one.

She would always remember the day, her first week at college, when she stood on the precipice of a decision in the dining hall. In front of her were three tables with people she knew. Two consisted of freshmen, Black like her, but also not like her at all. One was a table of Caribbean and African girls from Brooklyn with elaborate hair and clothing styles from the future; the other was full of African Americans from country club schools on the Main Line. She knew neither group would shun her outright, but that was not the same as a welcome. She knew they would not make it easy.

She sat down at the third table, filled with friendly and hairy white upperclassmen. They had been waving wildly at her, having assumed she was one of their own. And so it was that almost as soon as Liselle had set foot on the campus, she was being openly pursued by a girl named Manda, who looked like a boy band singer. Without feeling as if it answered any ancient or deep need in her, Liselle went along for the ride. In her former life as a straight person, she had heard tales of unsuspecting men and women being "recruited" by gays, which was literally homophobic and deeply offensive. And yet when she reflected on what had happened to her at the beginning of college, she felt it wasn't a terribly inapt description.

A month later, she was unceremoniously dumped by Manda, who had developed a serious cocaine problem and was collected one day by her horsey-looking parents in a blindingly white sports car that could scarcely contain her things. After Manda, there were, in quick succession, a brown girl from Bangladesh by way of California with hazel eyes; a sexy, fat, rich Black girl from New Hampshire; and, of course, a variety of white girls. There were so many willing and available white girls, getting their sticky hair tangled up in your sweaters, suffusing your small dorm room with their smell; she recalled a TV movie comedy where a Black woman who reminded her of Verity described white people as smelling like "wet potato chips." Of course, that wasn't *always* true.

As the only Black girl who ran with the boldest dykes—the ones who performed pornographic poems at coffee shops, a group that had reportedly kidnapped a Haverford College rapist, beat him up, and left him in the woods—she felt special. When sleeping her way through that clique started to get old, she finally "settled down" as a junior with a much-sought-after girl named Kit, her first real girl-friend. Around that time, she made a proclamation to Verity about "loving women." ("It was obvious what you were up to; you could have kept that announcement to yourself," her mother said years later.)

At the beginning of her last year, Liselle realized she had been a person of distinction among these small-time (mostly) white lesbians, and she suspected she would not likely be something again.

6 ⊚⊙

on was the first to arrive at the party, which was often the case. He was precise and detail-oriented; both his handsome brown shoes and his wheat-colored hair looked waxed. He generally took his time removing his aviator sunglasses once he was indoors. Often he reminded Liselle of the villain in the *Titanic* movie. He was unfailingly polite but not thoughtful, calling Xochitl "Señorita" as she let him in. Liselle knew Xochitl must hate that. But she was afraid to correct him and risk mispronouncing Xochitl's name.

"How are you doing, Ron?" Liselle attempted to sound brightly neutral, accepting a bouquet of flowers. His were always expensive and tasteful. This time there were purple calla lilies ringed with something golden, which made her tulips look tired.

"How am I doing?" he repeated, cocking his head. Liselle often recalled that he had once described himself as "just white, nothing fancy." The light glinted off his sunglasses and he touched them gently, still not ready to take them off. "I'm still drawing breath. I'm still in the fight."

Ron was a money manager who lived in a not-too-ostentatious home in Chestnut Hill. He had twin teenage daughters, track stars at their exclusive prep school. His wife was a pediatrician. And yet he was always saying things like, *I'm still in the fight; I won't let them get me down. I thank God for every day*, as if he were the survivor of a chronic illness, or a political prisoner. This confused Liselle and gave him, as far as she was concerned, a criminal air.

On his heels was Vanessa Sayre-Thomason, frequently the only other Black woman at VIP-type campaign affairs. "Hello, love," she said, pulling Liselle in for a substantial hug. She wore a soft sweater dress the coral color of which made Liselle ache with jealousy and desire. Also painful were Vanessa's small diamond earrings, her stainless steel men's watch, her shiny bob that looked like it might even be her real hair, and her lovely breast-to-hip ratio. When they'd met, a year and a half ago, Liselle had felt attracted to her, while also feeling that she looked familiar. Finally, she realized that Vanessa was Herself, the version she had imagined on a victory stage, smiling and waving by Winn's side.

"Hi," Liselle said shyly, as was her habit.

"Well, hello, *Vanessa*," said Winn. As usual, it darted through Liselle's mind that perhaps her husband was also attracted to Vanessa.

Embracing Winn, Vanessa said, "Phillip sends his regrets. But really," she continued in a faux-conspiratorial tone, "and I hope God doesn't strike me down for saying this, my husband is not exactly the life of the party. In fact, I would venture to say he is the proud *death* of many parties." Her laugh was low and striking; she deployed it a lot.

Liselle smiled weakly at the thought of the husband, who liked to toss out "A Modest Proposal"–type schemes to keep conversations interesting to him, regardless of how his interlocutors felt. At one campaign fundraiser, he had spent the night telling anyone who would listen about his plan for a massive reparations program that would include royalties paid to all Black people for the sale of fried chicken anywhere in the United States.

Besides the obnoxious husband, with whom Vanessa claimed she was "saving the world one check at a time," the only thing about her, the only catch, was the powerful rotten smell of her breath, so rich it was almost intriguing.

"Does she kiss her mother with that mouth?" Liselle had once joked to Winn. He had looked at her oddly, claiming he could not smell it. It was one of those small disjunctions of experience between them that made her feel gaslighted.

Liselle appraised the placement of cured olives and pepper crackers on side tables. Winn stood at the antique oak sideboard, nodding at Ron and mixing a drink. The thought of the sideboard tugged at Liselle. Ever since she was a girl and had heard someone on one of Verity's soap operas say "sideboard," she had wanted one. This piece of furniture had been in Winn's father's family since the 1700s, though the family had come close, several times, to selling it or burning it for firewood. Liselle remembered the last time she'd seen Winn's father, in a posh senior facility, sitting by the window looking confused. Only Patrice, who had a surprising solidity about him at times, was able to be patient, kind, and unsentimental with Mr. Anderson. Liselle was momentarily wounded by the image of an unlikely scene: Patrice trying to explain to his grandfather Winn's imprisonment and the resulting loss of the sideboard.

The doorbell continued to ring and Liselle decided she would not worry about who might show up that night. There seemed to be no good reason to haul Winn away during or after the dinner hour. As the party guests began to fill the sitting room, Gladys Banfield, a girlhood friend of Winn's long-dead mother, arrived.

"I'm so happy to see you all," she said as Liselle gave her a delicate hug. "Though I do need a word before the night is through."

"All ears," said Liselle, lapsing into the corny shorthand she spoke only at events like this or during her five minutes on the campaign "trail." Not long after, she greeted Ivelisse Peña with an ironic smile. "Are you allowed to be here?"

Ivelisse laughed. "What's up, Mama?" Though she had worked on Winn's primary campaign, she'd been snapped up by Church Williams for the general election. While the Williams victory was a sure thing in the historically Democratic district, hiring her had been part of a strategy to make nice with the new people on the scene, Winn's allies who'd worked to dislodge Williams from office. This was necessary, since he clearly wanted to hold the office forever.

"We can start planning the coup, baby," Ivelisse said with a wink.

Now here were Liza and Gary Appleton, a two-headed unit of unfashionable prescription lenses, new fleece, and wiry salt-and-pepper hair. "Are we all right?" asked Liza.

Liselle froze in panicked confusion. Then she remembered the loss of the election, which seemed laughable as a problem, considering that her husband might go to prison. "Oh yeah, of course."

"We're all right!" Liza hugged Liselle. "Of course we are."

"Easy, Liza," Gary said.

"I'm just asking if she's—"

"Probably she's doing even better when people aren't asking her how she's doing. Who wants to answer that question all the time? Did you like answering that question all the time after your—"

"I'm so glad to see you both," Liselle said, which was true. These were the only two people who would come tonight who'd originally been *her* friends. They had made several large donations to Winn's campaign, not because they were especially civic-minded, nor because they enjoyed the perks of money politics. They had instead been motivated by some decades-long zoning beef with Church Williams, the details of which were intricate and hard to follow.

Liselle had met Liza and Gary when she was teaching their son, Franklin, who had been smart enough, but not especially interested in school. After he nearly failed eighth grade, his parents had tried to play hardball by yanking him out of Quaker Academy and sending him to the 97 percent Black and 70 percent reduced-price-or-free-lunch high school in the neighborhood. He'd thwarted them by loving it. He could be seen around the neighborhood wearing an Africa medallion and saying "positivity" a lot. Beating the odds of his birth and station, he'd become the prom king at Douglass High.

"How's Franklin?" Liselle asked. The answer was a hoarse barking sound from Liza.

"Liza," Gary said, "lately I've been noticing you make that noise when someone asks after our son. Maybe the fact that you've never taken him seriously is part of the reason why he's in the situation he's in."

This was not an especially dramatic exchange between them. To Liselle's relief, Liza and Gary never did the rich-people thing of over-respecting boundaries or observing propriety. The people she'd grown up with, principally her mother, didn't give a fuck about your boundaries because what were you trying to hide? Liselle remembered once complaining of a stomachache in order to shorten a tedious trip to Pathmark. "When's the last time you moved your bowels?" Verity had asked in her sonorous voice.

"Gary, do I understand you to be saying that my laughing is the reason he dropped out of BU and is living in a cabin in North Carolina without another Jewish individual in a hundred-mile radius? You think he's devoted his life to studying the banjo with toothless hill folk because I laugh at him?"

Liselle covered her mouth.

"*You* can laugh, Liselle," Gary said. "Go ahead. You're not his mother."

Then Winn was there and apparently had been for some time. "You know, I get it," he said, shaking his head. "I totally get what Franklin is doing. When I was his age, I just created another world and then lived in it. It's part of being a young man."

Something about that rankled Liselle, but she couldn't be bothered to uncover it. Then she remembered something she'd forgotten until this moment. "Winn, remember when you were going to get a fishing boat in Mexico?"

"That's right. I had read *The Old Man and the Sea*," he said, with a performative melancholy that may or may not have been covering up genuine sadness. Liselle didn't mention that the Hemingway novel took place in Cuba or remind him of the ending.

"I *wish* Franklin were down in Mexico. *There* we would visit! Do you know he gets his water from a well? I'm just waiting for the call when he tells me he has a parasite. I mean, I guess the water's not better in Mexico—"

Winn glanced at Liselle and then gently touched Liza's shoulder. "Liza, all this talk of drinking reminds me that you enjoy a dirty martini. Shall we?"

"How is Patrice doing?" Gary asked Liselle after Winn gently steered Liza to the other side of the room. "He must be happy the campaign is over."

"He's fine." *For now*, she thought. "He's happy," she continued, though it was a funny word to use about Patrice in any case. He wasn't an *unhappy* child; he was just Patrice, the way she had been herself as a child. "He didn't really want us to win. He likes the status quo—or, I should say, he prefers it." She pushed away the memory of an age-inappropriate tantrum when he'd ripped a stack of campaign pamphlets to shreds, assaulting the smiling family portraits and yelling, "Who are these people?"

Gary sighed. "Well, then."

"Well, then," replied Liselle. She'd read somewhere that sighing was a habit marked female, like fainting.

Liza and Gary would still be her friends, she thought, when they learned Winn was being accused of a crime. She glanced with some longing at Ivelisse with her perfect brows and naturally straight hair, which Liselle suspected she ironed ever straighter. She'd never see her or Vanessa again.

When Liselle's mind traveled back to the room, Gary was saying, ". . . ever gonna go back to teaching? No matter what a confusing work of art Franklin is determined to make out of his life, you were one of the good things that happened in his education. I always remember how excited he was about your class."

"Thank you, Gary," said Liselle. He had said as much before, but the fact of how often he repeated it meant he was not lying. She felt moved, but also regretful. She had been a good teacher; people had always said so. But she had never really cared about it. It was hard to remember what she'd wanted to be. Maybe just comfortable and happy.

Xochitl stood expectantly in the doorway, a sign to move into the dining room.

7

The good news about the final year of college was that there was a class about Black women writers, taught by a new Black woman prof. When Liselle arrived, she realized with a sinking feeling that the excitement was widespread.

The room buzzed with too many bodies, too many girls flushed pink with excitement. Chairs wrapped and double-wrapped the long table. Liselle felt her shoulders gripping for the fight to stay in the class, which would likely prioritize English majors. Though she loved novels, she had not majored in literature. Her freshman writing seminar had been taught by a white man in his seventies who smelled like cigars and mulch and believed World War I was and would always be the most significant event in world history. He'd given Liselle her first and only C. She'd landed in anthropology largely because the intro class, though also taught by an aged white man, had included *Mules and Men*.

"This class is called Writing a Way from No Way. I don't even think we need to talk about why, but eventually we will," announced Professor Bruin, a tall, slender woman with sharp cheekbones and a tall fade haircut. She wore a collared white shirt, brown slacks, and lace-up oxford shoes. After roll call, during which it was established that most people in the room were on the wait list, class began with

an icebreaker. Everyone took turns saying their name and mentioning the last book they'd "enjoyed." A shrill girl who'd waved her hand
around obnoxiously back in freshman seminar claimed she'd read
Das Kapital. A student whom Liselle knew to be a combination of
punk and teacher's pet, with her three face piercings and obscene
T-shirt, said she was "like totally obsessed with Didion." Liselle panicked; she hadn't read anything all summer. She and Kit, her ex, had
worked, fucked, and lain in front of the television in a cross section
of fans blowing hot air around.

"*Tropic of Cancer,*" blurted Liselle. It was a book she knew nothing about; she had seen it, two copies, actually, side by side in the
place where she and Kit had been house-sitting. Tittering erupted,
and it struck Liselle that she and the professor were the only two
Black women there. Didn't other Black girls at Bryn Mawr want to
read books by Black women? As if on cue, the classroom door burst
open.

The arriving girl was, Liselle could see without even turning her
head, Black, and wearing something skimpy and bright yellow—all
wrong for showing up late. Liselle felt her cheeks warm as the girl
clacked forward in what sounded like platform shoes.

As the class continued to casually demonstrate their erudite and
wide-ranging tastes, Liselle began to feel she might very well hate,
if not this professor, then her fawning white familiars. Though
the names on the syllabus thrilled her—Ntozake Shange, Audre
Lorde, Octavia Butler, Angela Davis, Lucille Clifton, Jayne Cortez
(an unfamiliar, lovely name)—she reflected that on the first day of
class, it was permissible to get up and quietly leave. She could give
her seat to the girl standing near the door in her ridiculous dress.

"Miss," said the professor, "before you arrived, we were introducing ourselves and sharing the title of something we enjoyed reading
recently."

Selena Octave had recently enjoyed reading *The Coldest Winter*

Ever by Sister Souljah. The class looked to the clearly bemused professor for guidance. Verity had hated that book, but it had made a strong impression on Liselle . . . especially some parts. Liselle looked at Selena, her short, ropy dreadlocks, lips like Lauryn Hill's. Remembering that *The Coldest Winter Ever* had given Liselle what Kit called a "girl boner," she forgot to get up and leave the class.

She couldn't stop staring at Selena.

Liselle had had some notable first encounters. When she met Manda, she had imagined them tangled up in each other. At the party where she met Kit, she'd felt a charge that could just as easily have been violent dislike. Between those years, the pull Liselle felt to various girls had been primarily about their thereness. She wondered if this girl was gay, feeling panic and dread at either possibility.

After Professor Bruin dismissed the class, a throng of students moved toward her to make the case for why they needed to take the course. Liselle moved against the flow, instead heading toward Selena, so intently thinking of what she would say that she didn't see the monogrammed tote bag in her path. Though at one point she had been falling forward, she somehow wound up on her back.

"Are you okay?" Liselle looked up into liquid black eyes, smoky with kohl, wide with worry. She had magnificent eyebrows; though the style at that time was thin little half-moons, her thick, neatly shaped ones shined with luster. Slender gold bracelets tinkled as she reached out and touched Liselle on the shoulder.

"I'm fine," said Liselle. Then a throbbing in her head made her lie back down. A phrase from Verity's favorite book by Toni Morrison popped into Liselle's head: "a hot thing."

The girl squatted, folding her impossibly long legs. "Liselle, right?"

Professor Bruin stood over the two of them. "Maybe you should stop by the infirmary just to be sure? I think I heard your head hit the floor." To Selena, she said, "You'll look after her, won't you?"

"Am I in the class?" Liselle asked, but the throng of white girls had already closed around the professor again.

"Can you stand?" the girl asked as she helped Liselle up.

"Of course," Liselle said, though she was unsure until she was on her feet. Then she tried to play cool. "Do you have somewhere to be? I think I can make it there on my own."

Selena dismissed that with a wave. "I'm done with classes for the day. But I don't know where the infirmary is, so if you're strong enough you'll have to lead us there."

It was a soft afternoon, temperamentally more late June than early September. The campus had a dreamy green aura.

"How do you walk in those shoes?" she asked, looking at Selena's stacked Mary Janes. It was not what she had imagined herself saying, but she was panicked at the silence. She had not felt anxious around someone in this way for years.

Selena smiled, looking down at Liselle's Doc Martens. "I'm not the one who just did a somersault."

Liselle laughed. "Ouch."

"Yes, I believe that is what you said when you fell too."

Considering it was the first day of classes, the waiting room was surprisingly full of the infirm; at least one girl was sobbing quietly. The wait was long enough for them to learn they were both from Philadelphia, which for reasons Liselle never understood was not common among the Black girls on campus. Liselle hailed from West Philadelphia, Selena from farther west. They had gone to different academic magnet high schools.

While making small talk, Liselle made calculations: this girl was new to college. After she stopped running around with the ill-conceived crew she had picked up during freshman orientation, she would need actual friends. But was this the beginning of a friendship? She looked at Selena's lips, the small shapes of her collarbone, moist with sweat, and felt like a lesbian vampire, also light-headed. Maybe these were concussion symptoms.

Liselle thought ruefully of Kit, the first girl to say "I love you." She had dutifully parroted it back less than three months ago. Early in the summer she *had* felt love, house-sitting in a gorgeous downtown apartment belonging to a gay couple that were family friends of Kit's parents. But deep into July, Liselle had wondered aloud one too many times why people who could afford air conditioners didn't have them, and drunkenly set off a three-hour argument by describing a café waitress as beguiling. It was during that argument that Kit had pried it out of Liselle that she did not and could never love Kit.

"Or maybe anyone, really," she'd said, at which Kit had laughed maniacally and then hurled a bunch of words at Liselle that stung: "damaged," "user," "social climber," "empty hole where your heart should be."

Liselle had waited until the last possible day to come back to campus from Verity's house, feeling both shame and paranoia about the whole thing. She pledged to stay away from girls and devote herself to her studies, her future, and becoming a better person. Now she was chatting up this freshman girl who was probably straight, even if their arms lightly rested against each other as they sat side by side in boxy wood chairs. Kit's rage, her pronouncement, the vow to stay away from girls, the blazing sight of Selena; she ran through cycles of these thoughts in the span of a few minutes. Then she screwed up her courage as if to jump into freezing water.

Liselle smiled. "I can't believe your boyfriend didn't want to go to the same college to keep an eye on you."

Here there was a pause during which she died while Selena busied herself untangling her thin bracelets. She (finally) looked up.

"I don't have a boyfriend," she said. Her eyes were sad; the effect as she smiled was of sunshine through rain, rainbows. "What about *your* boyfriend? How does he deal with the distance?"

They looked at each other.

"Why are you laughing?"

"Why are *you* laughing?"

8

They were already seated at the dining room table over spiky greens when Reverend Chris arrived, late as usual, doused in cologne: baby powder with a kerosene edge.

"Y'all up here eating unblessed salad?" he said in the ironic voice he used for everything except preaching.

Winn barked his name happily.

"Rev," Liselle said. She felt a grudging affection toward him. He had been drafted into the campaign's inner circle for the usual cynical reasons white candidates dragged Black clergy into their ciphers, but even more cynical—silly, even—considering that it seemed to be part of a strategy for beating a candidate named Church.

It had not worked, but there was something about Chris, many things, in fact, that made him interesting to Liselle. He was not even *that* light-skinned, but he had freckles. His dreadlocks were always arranged in a confusing fashion, piled atop his head like sculpture. He dressed like a B-boy, with a heavy swinging chain, a *Jesus piece*, in fact, and sagging (expensive-looking) jeans. He was, however, in his thirties, a married father of three children. And she knew without knowing that he was gay.

"Where did they get this clown?" Liselle had muttered to Winn the first time she saw him, at a community center event. Directly after having been introduced, Chris had burst into the song "Love's in Need of Love Today." Liselle had continued to glare, despite the fact that his voice sounded like honey, velvet, Gabriel's trumpet. When it ended, she felt like weeping.

Then he spoke, and this was the weird part.

Listening to him, Liselle felt recognized, affirmed, exhorted to claim her true place in the world, and, glancing furtively at other people in the room, she knew they felt it too. But as soon as he stopped speaking, she could not remember a single thing he'd said. That was the first of many times she would hear him addressing people at events, offering benedictions, introducing Winn, or testifying his support. The same thing always happened afterward. His words evaporated.

It reminded her of being in college, reading long theoretical articles, feeling she understood them at a molecular level, but later finding herself unable to reconstruct their central arguments. Once, she'd queried Winn to see if he was having the same problem with the reverend, but he began to blush just at the mention of his name. "Isn't he just amazing?"

"Yes," Liselle had said, "but . . ."

"There is always a big 'but' with you," Winn had said dryly. "It's a wonder I managed to slip past your big 'but's into this marriage."

"I'm just going to say some quick words, if you don't mind," said Chris, standing awkwardly at his place at the table while the others sat. He improvised a grace that struck Liselle as unnecessarily layered and lengthy for an event with so many white guests. His voice cast a spell like a beautiful piece of sad music; Liselle was reminded of a certain quality of light. Finally, he said, "Amen."

Then everything he'd said was gone.

Winn was beaming and Ron Mack grunted his approval. "As always, you make me want to renounce my lifelong Episcopal situation," he said.

"As always, the doors of Ezekiel Baptist are open to you," Chris said (ironically).

"You say that, but seriously. I'm telling you, the family is coming up there next Sunday. You will see me in the front pew. Me, the missus, the girls, we are *there*."

Poking at her salad with feigned interest, Liselle heard a snort. Vanessa.

"Everything okay, Van?" Ron grinned.

"I'm sorry," she said, laughing as if she couldn't stop when it was obvious she could. It was the thing she did that most reminded Liselle of the annoying husband.

"Ron," she said, "don't mind me, but outside of a couple of campaign stops, have you ever gotten out of the car in North Philly? I know you're just trying to be polite, but, like, for months we've been listening to you say you're going to that church and it's so . . ." Here she fake capsized with fake laughter.

Liselle disliked when Vanessa did this, resorted to forced laughter in order to say something mildly aggressive or confrontational. And yet as she watched Ron's eyes narrowing, she suddenly felt gratitude. There was so much lying all the time, particularly when you got together with people who were not Black. Bland observations about schools, neighborhoods, and the words "kids" and "safe" and "family" tried to cover up a landscape of volcanos oozing with blood, pus, and shit. It was not always clear to Liselle what occasionally pushed someone over the edge into simply stating the truth, but when she or someone else did it, as tense as it was in the moment, she usually experienced relief later.

"Come on, Vanessa," said Winn. "Stop breaking balls."

Ron's smile was stiff. "Actually, Vanessa, my grandfather owned some properties up in the Strawberry Mansion area even after . . . it changed. Also, remember that I'm a graduate of Temple University—"

"Go, Owls," said Chris, unbothered and eating mushroom puffs, though the discussion at hand was nominally about his rather shabby church, which Liselle knew sat perpendicular to a thriving open-air drug market.

"As a matter of fact," Ron continued, "the fraternity house where I lived . . ."

"You lived in a *fraternity house* in North Philly?" asked Ivelisse, which ended the difficult part of the conversation because everyone laughed, including Ron. "Are you sure it even was a fraternity house? Because my mom had to drag my uncle out of some different spots around there where there was a lot of partying, but I never heard them called fraternity houses . . ."

"Ha, ha," Ron said.

Reverend Chris said, "The last two buildings my church leased were bought out from under us by Temple frats, which, if I'm being frank, were not much better for the neighborhood than the crack houses."

"At least the crack houses offered something the community wanted," Winn muttered.

Liselle felt a slight sense of alarm. This was not the kind of joke Winn usually made in mixed company. But the reverend chuckled. "Right. And then at least sometimes I would see people sweeping up in front of the crack house. On the other hand, the brothers of Sigma were not big community stewards. But crack house, frat house, rock and a hard place." He waved his hand, which was slender and bejeweled.

"Now, I wonder what you could mean by that," said Gladys. She did not speak a lot at these events, but every now and then she clicked into the room for good or for ill. "You're joking, right?"

"Not really, Ms. Gladys," said Chris in a kind voice.

"But how could drug addicts be better neighbors than a house full of college students?"

"*Gentrification.*" Gary spoke at the top of his voice, apparently for Gladys's benefit. Liza had told Liselle that Gary was phobic about the elderly. He yelled in the faces of people who were not hard of hearing, or explained things to them as if they were elementary school students. If a person with a cane or even a slow shuffle headed toward him on the street, he preferred to cross. Liselle wondered how he would handle turning sixty, which was not far off.

"When whites move in, they push Blacks out," he yelled in Gladys's general direction. Liza wore a mortified expression.

Gladys smiled as if addressing one of the more dim-witted subjects in her royal court. "Yes, but Black, white, or purple, who wants to live near a crack house?"

"Well, Aunt Gladys, I think it's a little more complicated than that," said Winn. Though he often complained about her cluelessness, he had worked to keep his mother's friend in their lives. He claimed it was out of pity, but she had been a financial resource on a number of occasions. As Gladys began explaining the drawbacks of living near crack addicts, Winn looked meaningfully at Liselle. *Fix this.*

"Table question!" she announced. Everyone groaned with delight. This was her one dinner amusement move, not so different, she thought, from Fuck, Marry, Kill, a favorite from early days with Winn. Previous table questions with this group had included "What's the craziest thing you've done with a baby in your arms?" (Ivelisse had gotten into a fistfight with her sister-in-law) and "Which one person (yes, Hitler, but who else) should be eliminated from world history?" The Appletons had argued fiercely between them about the matter of Woodrow Wilson versus Frank Rizzo. Ron, who was one generation out of white South Philadelphia, had scoffed at the idea of eradicating Rizzo, coloring slightly. "Wasn't he a little local to make a difference in world history?" Ron himself was immovable on Osama bin Laden in answer to the question. The table thought that was a waste of a wish.

Liselle wrote down lists of these questions in a notebook where she kept track of things: Which religion would you observe if you had to take up religion or convert? Which one would you give up if you had to: music, movies, or books? If you could only ever eat one meal a day, which of the three would it be? Liselle once told the table about a movie in which Morgan Freeman plays a violent knife-wielding pimp who asks Christopher Reeve which eye he wants to lose. She joked about, but didn't ask, gross questions. Nor did she ask the questions she'd brainstormed that made her feel frightened and wistful: if you could change one thing about your life, if you could change one thing about the past.

"Let's hear it, Liselle," said Ron.

"Okay. What's your greatest fear that's also your stupidest?"

Vanessa clapped. "Oh, goody. Mine used to be a hanging slip before we all stopped wearing slips."

Gladys looked surprised. "Who stopped wearing slips?"

"Who ever started?" Liza retorted.

"Liza, you don't even wear skirts," Gary said. "You haven't worn a skirt since college."

"What are you so sad about? You're so sad, you wear a friggin' skirt. I still have one somewhere in the attic."

"Focus on the question," said Liselle. "Vanessa, since it can't be your nonexistent hanging slip, what *is* your most ridiculous constant fear?"

Weirdly, Ron raised his hand. "That I left the toilet seat up in my house."

"But it's your house," said Winn.

"Look, man, I live with three women. And once, when the twins were just learning to use the real toilet, Ashley slipped and sat her little tush in poop water. Jeanine's been yelling about it ever since. *Ronny,*" he said in a falsetto, "*this isn't the dog track!*"

"Oh, Ronny," said Ivelisse. "You go to the dog track?"

Gary blurted, "I worry about rising sea levels."

Winn sputtered, "Gary, that's not a stupid fear. That's a party killer."

"Fine," said Gary. "I worry I'm going to back over a child with my car."

Liza rolled her eyes theatrically. "What are you talking about? We haven't had a driveway since that awful house in Wilmington."

"It's just that every time I back up anywhere, I worry I won't see a child."

"Gary, have you had that checked out?" asked Liselle. "Maybe you *want* to run over a child. Your own child?"

The table had become merry. The key was to keep them laughing, and to limit the alcohol so the mood didn't crash in anticipation of the end of the night or a hungover morning. Jimena would have been through to refill both water and wineglasses until the bottles set out for the evening were gone. Xochitl was likely in the kitchen reading Noam Chomsky.

"When I was thirteen," Winn said, "I split my swimming trunks going off the diving board. Somehow that remains a concern, even when I'm not swimming."

"I worry I forgot to put on deodorant," said Ivelisse, "but it's really hard to smell your own armpits without anyone noticing."

"You smell amazing." Ron always wound up sitting next to Ivelisse. In response she lifted her arm. "How do you get your armpit to smell like cinnamon?" he asked. As occasionally happened, Chris and Liselle caught each other's eyes. More than the others, they were people-watchers.

Vanessa swirled her glass of cabernet in a way that was above its price point. "Well, now that there are no slips, I just worry that one day I'm going to wake up back in that tiny-ass shack in Jamaica where I used to spend summers with mean Tanty."

"I have never made it to Jamaica," said Gladys Banfield. "I would very much like to go. I've been to Bermuda but it wasn't a real Caribbean vacation. This time, I might like to eat the fruit there and have my hair braided like Bo Derek." She did, Liselle thought, have an enviably thick head of glossy silver hair.

"Well, dear," said Liza, looking at Vanessa. "One day we will all wake up in that tiny house in Jamaica with mean Tanty."

"In the sky," said Ron Mack.

"Under sea level," said Gary.

"What about you, Liselle?" Vanessa asked. "What silly thing do you fear?"

Liselle was thinking about what she had not feared. She had not feared a family case of political corruption, the FBI, or her family's disgrace. Many years ago, she had tried to disabuse Selena of the conviction that fear was a form of preparation. Now she wondered.

9 ◎◎

fter leaving the infirmary without seeing a doctor, Liselle and Selena spent their first weekend together, almost a solid forty-eight hours straight, in Liselle's dorm suite, alternating between the common room couch (being glared at by suite mates in transit) and the bedroom. Selena woke up Monday morning before 7:00 a.m., shivering, her skin burning to the touch. Lacking a thermometer, Liselle brought her tap water, which Selena gulped and declared delicious.

They had holed up that weekend talking, having sex, and taking quick trips to the cafeteria. They had made only token attempts at homework. Professor Bruin had assigned all of *The Street* for the second class, which Liselle knew to be a winnowing tactic. Eager to not be winnowed, she had read much of it in the night while Selena slept, but had been hoping to use Monday to finish.

"Um," she began.

"I know I should let you do your work and go to class," Selena said.

"No, you can stay here. It's totally fine," Liselle lied. "I'll go to the library and see what I can get done and come back with soup or something."

"Don't," whispered Selena. "Don't leave." The pitch of her voice suggested Liselle would make a run back to base while Selena would sacrifice herself to enemy forces. She made a sad puppy face and coughed.

"Girl, you don't have a cough," said Liselle. "But, fine, I'll stay here and we'll fail out together."

Liselle climbed back into bed and watched Selena drift off again. She looked like a breathtakingly beautiful doll, even wearing a little scowl. Liselle wondered how this doll-person had materialized on campus and almost immediately found her way into Liselle's bed. It was like the beginning of a parable: a parable or that Billy Ocean song.

Liselle suddenly felt afraid. She knew how girls were. She knew that in spending the weekend with Selena she might have inadvertently put a down payment on a future she was not ready to ante up. She thought about what she'd said, and meant, to Kit. She thought about what Kit had said to her. As she grew drowsier, she imagined Verity's disapproving face.

The next time they were both awake, sun blazed into the room. Selena pulled herself up and sat cross-legged on the bed, looking less frail. She grinned.

"Hey, Liselle," she said, "you know what they call you, right?"

"They who?"

"The dykes."

"The white ones?"

"Aren't we the only Black ones?"

"The only ones who'll admit to it, I guess."

"You mean the ones who will admit to being Black?"

"Fuck do I care what they call me?" said Liselle, who was dying to know.

Selena said, "The Wolf."

Liselle rolled her eyes theatrically and made a noise in her throat. "Who is saying this? And who is talking to freshmen about me?"

Selena frowned, remembering. "Well, there was a story about a girl named Dawn? And then her roommate?"

"It's so stupid here!" Liselle cried. Yes, she had slept with Dawn, but Dawn was a heroine in her own opera of the closet, featuring her racist parents in suburban New Jersey. She was not sexy enough for it not to be boring. And, yes, the next semester after a party Liselle had stumbled home with Dawn's roommate, whose name was either Alexa or Alison; she couldn't quite remember because the girl had quickly transferred. But all the lesbians slept with all the lesbians, as far as she could see, because despite the school's reputation, there weren't quite enough of them. She didn't say this to Selena.

"Where did you learn all of this? Orientation?" Liselle asked.

"Did you start your hunting at orientation?" asked Selena, playing a little game on Liselle's arm. "Should I be scared?"

Liselle stood abruptly. "I'm gonna shower." But instead she stood there, arms folded, staring angrily at a wall. "The Wolf." It could have flattered her vanity, but it was absurd. This idea of her as a cruel seducer was just a way of marking her as Black by women who were supposed to be sisters and comrades. And this kind of thing was exactly why she suspected that one day they would marry men, move to the suburbs, and stash their diaries in family heirloom chests with ski sweaters. Vote Republican.

"Don't be salty," Selena said. "I thought you knew."

"I'm not salty," Liselle snapped. "And you're pretty lively for somebody who was dying a few hours ago."

Selena's lovely face crumpled, filling Liselle with panic.

"No, it's okay," Liselle said. "I'm sorry. I know how two-faced these white girls are. It's just hard because I spend so much time with them."

"Well, I think it's kind of sexy. I wish I were a wolf," Selena said, biting her lip. She smiled then, her smile, which, Liselle was beginning to know, was always a sad one.

ochitl emerged from the kitchen and began clearing plates. Liselle stood officiously to help. "It's really okay," murmured Xochitl, so she sat back down.

"My greatest fear," said Liselle, "is that my true feelings about dinner parties will become known."

"That's so funny, Liselle," said Ivelisse. The way she said *thas* made Liselle feel comfortable. "You throw a lot of really nice ones."

"It's a struggle. My beginnings were humble."

Dinner parties were not a thing people like Verity did. Sometimes Aunt Bizzy, Verity's much older sister by another father, had come over. "Want some food?" Verity would ask her. Or Mr. Charles, Verity's on-and-off boyfriend-chauffeur, might join them in front of the TV with food on his lap, beers for him and Verity. Once, Liselle and Winn had invited Verity and Mr. Charles for dinner when Winn's parents were in town. It was a night of multifaceted awkwardness. Liselle had been trapped between Winn's parents' complaints about the portions of food (too large) and Verity's angry discomfort at such a formal event in someone's home.

As Liselle regarded her table, which shined like a spread in a food magazine, with Ron's superior floral arrangement casually in the center (relegating hers to the kitchen), she laughed aloud thinking about a time she had been so intoxicated with her newly refined tastes that she tried to serve her mother and her mother's sometime boyfriend beef tartare. Then she remembered once again that her husband was going to be arrested and her life was going to become a museum of shame that her mother (and Mr. Charles) would be able to visit.

"What's funny?" asked Vanessa.

"Just a joke between me and myself."

"The best kind," Vanessa said, laughing demonstratively.

"It's usually so jammed up in here," said Ron. "I finally get to spread out and show you all my salt of the earth manners," he said, resting his elbows on the table.

For some self-sabotaging reason, Liselle had not asked for firm RSVPs for this dinner. She did that sometimes: became anxious about something and let it fester. Sitting at the half-empty table in the dining room as Xochitl cleared the salad, she realized that the best example of this tendency in her was life with Winn. Case in point: when she had begun wondering about the sustainability of her marriage, she responded not by talking about it with him or anyone else—but by taking lengthy drives along the crazy twists of Lincoln Drive, both enjoying the beautiful scenery and feeling nihilistic. When he came up with the attention-diverting idea to run for office, she'd gratefully put her doubts on hold.

Ron sat at Winn's side. "Jeanine sends her regards, by the way. She's at home with the girls."

Chris and Vanessa had left their spouses at home, too—surprising, since both loved parties, but Ron's wife was never around. Still, each time she was absent, Ron reported what she was supposedly doing. Liselle wondered with unease why he was always making excuses on her behalf; she certainly wasn't at home babysitting two sixteen-year-olds.

Winn spoke, interrupting Liselle's vision of Jeanine's corpse on the rocks of the Wissahickon. "Honey, maybe we should take the extender out of the table. All of this empty space at the table makes me feel . . ." He trailed off. It was true that there was a missing-tooth effect to some of the table spacing, as guests had opted not to sit on top of one another. And yet the table was full of intricate place settings and a meal in progress. Winn's suggestion of removing the extender leaf at this point was absurd. How on earth would he have been an effective politician with these problem-solving skills?

And he'd called her *honey*, which he did only in front of other people. The first time he'd done that, at his parents' Gothic storybook house in the West End of Hartford, it had felt like a threat. Then it became a joke between them. One day he seemed to have forgotten the joke part.

"You should do whatever you think is good," Liselle said, knowing it would displease him. Winn liked to float his general feelings about a domestic situation to goad her into making the decisions and taking the action.

"Whatever I think is good," he repeated.

Liselle stood abruptly, knocking the table with her knees, sloshing some water from the cut glass pitcher. *Yes, Winn, by all means, let's rearrange the deck chairs.* "Can everybody move down this way?" she said. There was some obedient shuffling and confusion about whose glass belonged to whom. "I haven't worn lipstick since nineteen eighty-two, sweetie," Liza was saying to Vanessa, "so I'm pretty sure that's yours." Vanessa laughed. Liselle sometimes tried to fantasize about sex with Vanessa, but then she'd remember her breath.

"Do you want me to take away these extra place settings before the next course?" Xochitl asked. Just then the doorbell rang.

Winn smiled. "Not so fast," he said, a shade of triumph in his voice.

"I really think this is it for guests, actually," Liselle said, feeling shaky.

Xochitl stood holding a plate in midair. "Uh—"

"I'll get it," Liselle said.

"Why not let—this young lady get it?" Winn asked.

"Stay here," said Liselle, now sure she should have canceled the fucking party.

A large-framed woman stood on the porch in a stained green windbreaker. Though the night was chilly, her blackberry-colored face glistened with sweat under a rumpled maroon-colored wig. She was picturesque in an abject way, like a subject in an edgy photo exhibit about city life.

"Ma'am, I was just noticing your windows could use a bit of a shine. Wondering if maybe I could wipe them down for a couple of dollars."

Relief that the woman was not two men in mid-priced suits with briefcases gave way to a mix of irritation and guilt. "It's not a good time," said Liselle. "I'm having a—" She caught herself before she told the woman she was hosting a dinner party, but not before she felt a sharp pang of self-loathing about it.

"Miss, I'm not begging. I work. I'm just trying to feed my children. I did the windows for the lady up the street. The big place on the corner up the street," she repeated, and gestured loosely.

"Now is not a good time," Liselle repeated, gripping the door-nob, wondering about the woman's age and if any children were actually in her care. Then she recalled a man who'd rung the bell to their previous house one evening after dark many years ago; it had been just her and baby Patrice, as they often were in those days while Winn was out with clients catching martinis for billable hours. She had been sitting on the couch nursing, with the blinds drawn. On such occasions, the ringing doorbell already felt like an emergency. Where to put the baby/how to cover her boob/with what to clean up the drip?

The man who'd been at the door all those years ago had worn

the same expression as this woman. When Liselle had come out onto her small porch to say she was sorry, she didn't have anything for him, she felt him looming, tall and barrel-chested. As he was turning to walk away, he'd done a double take, his eyes frantic, disbelieving and full of rage. "I'm trying to do right," he'd said.

She, Winn, and the baby had lived closer to Germantown back then, and Germantown was basically North Philly. The incident had helped Liselle make the case that they needed to move to a nicer block, farther toward Chestnut Hill, but not in Chestnut Hill, where Liselle herself often felt like a panhandler.

That run-in had seemed like a big deal then; it happened more these days, at least twice in this house, this year, people who looked desperate ringing the bell. Liselle found it unsettling, also incongruent. Every day she read in the news about something wonderful happening in America. After centuries of genocide and subjugation, here was a Muslim holiday being celebrated at the White House or a marginal and hurt person going on a celebratory book tour; there was a round, gap-toothed Black woman who looked like everybody's aunt running multiple scripted television shows with huge budgets.

On Liselle's porch, the woman turned to go and then looked back, sucking her teeth loudly.

"I'm sorry," said Liselle.

"Have a blessed day," the woman intoned robotically. Then she was gone more swiftly than Liselle would have thought, melting into darkness.

A sudden hand on her shoulder. "Liselle," said Winn. "Shut the door." She was slow in responding to him, though she had the feeling she should move quickly, that time was running out.

◎◎ **11** ◎◎

"ook," Selena had said, staring over Liselle's shoulder in the general direction of the salad bar, "maybe it's not happening now, but it happened."

They were in the cafeteria a week after their first "date" at the infirmary. Though she hated to dampen the celebratory mood, Selena thought it was time to explain herself to Liselle.

There were times, she advised, that she wouldn't answer her phone. There were times when she might turn numb and frightened. She could not watch TV news. Her plan was to avoid history classes at college.

"What are we talking about," asked Liselle. "Depression?"

"Not quite," said Selena.

Like so many things, it started with Christopher Columbus.

The year Selena started kindergarten, her working parents dropped her with Aunt Braxton, on the Columbus Day school holiday. Aunt Braxton styled hair in her home, near Fifteenth and Diamond, before she could afford a salon, and Selena loved the house and its smells of thick petroleum jelly and burned coconuts. Too, she adored Aunt Braxton, who had a sharp, ever-changing coif and an impeccable manicure, and implicitly dared anyone to say anything to her about her relatively lush salt-and-pepper beard.

Unlike Selena's parents, who clutched their emotions tightly, Aunt Braxton was often openly angry. Selena loved listening to her rail against her "good-time gang" North Philadelphia neighbors, their "no home training" kids, rude salespeople, and, of course, white people in general and specifically. Listening to her mother describe Aunt Braxton's rants was how Selena learned the word "monologue." Today Aunt Braxton was angry that Selena was there. "Like chasing around my own kids ain't enough. Like working from eight a.m. till dark ain't enough, I got to work *and* watch other people's children."

"Yeah, it's a lot," the woman in the styling chair agreed. "But they family. And they good kids." She winked at Selena, who was cozy on the plastic-covered couch between her twin cousins, Pater and Seraphim.

"Hmph. They all gotta be fed and watered," said Aunt Braxton. Selena knew that Pater and Seraphim weren't listening. They couldn't hear anything else when the TV was on, whether it was reruns of their favorite, *The Munsters*, or ads for trucking school.

"I'm sorry," Selena said finally. But she wasn't. She was happy to be there.

"Oh no, it's not *your* fault, baby," said Aunt Braxton, using a thin comb to part the woman's forest of hair. She would transform it into a miraculous series of shining sheets. As usual, Selena was entranced; she touched her own babyish cornrows scornfully. Her mouth watered at the idea that one day her mother would finally let Aunt Braxton straighten her hair.

"And anyway," Aunt Braxton complained, "Columbus Day is— excuse my language here—some *bull*shit."

Selena loved the way she drew out the word: *bouuuuuul*shit.

"I mean, you tell me," she continued, "why on earth my Black ass should be celebrating Columbus?"

Then Aunt Braxton, as was her custom, began to answer herself.

There was no reason to celebrate Columbus, who had unleashed white people on the innocent, nature-loving people of the Americas. As she spoke, Selena could see the reddish-brown natives with bright black eyes and beautiful straight hair (*Indian* hair, as they said at school) clutching infected blankets, waking up covered in exploding sores. She saw long lines of them forced from their tepees, trudging across the snow in thin moccasins, at the end of a dirty white man's rifle. Selena thought of how kids claimed to have Indian blood, which was clearly more special than being all-Black or even part-white; clearly no one had told them about all this.

For the rest of that day at Aunt Braxton's, Selena went through the motions in the argument with her cousins over whether they should play Uno or hide-and-seek; she choked down the peanut butter sandwich she was given for lunch, and managed to win a couple of hands of War. But her mind kept slipping back to the malicious blankets, the long walk. She imagined her own feet, burning after playing in the snow too long the time when her boots had a secret hole.

"Braxton sure does like to run her mouth," her mother said that evening when Selena mentioned what she'd heard about Columbus, the Pilgrims, and the Indians. "She'll say anything in front of anybody."

"But is it true?" Selena asked.

"Well, yes," said Alethia smoothly. "But this was hundreds of years ago. People treated each other terribly back then. That was the way of the world."

"Oh yeah. Back then." Selena's father laughed behind the newspaper, a picture of the smiling president on the front page. Her parents despised him; her father deliberately mispronounced his name *Ray*-gun. Selena thought he was cute, like a big white monkey.

She tried to push Aunt Braxton's stories to the back of her mind.

It surely wasn't the first time she'd heard anything terrible. There was slavery, of course. And Jim Crow—every year in celebration of Black History Month, the news showed old-time footage of little Black children being fire-hosed and attacked with police dogs. That was some knowledge Selena felt she'd always had, as if she'd been inoculated as a toddler.

In contrast, the story of the Indians kept unfolding on the screen of her mind, especially when she lay down to sleep at night. At school she was able to focus mainly on the things she liked about her life: first-grade math with Ms. Gallagher, which consisted of playing with elegant, colorful wooden rods. This had changed the day before Thanksgiving that year. Selena's class took turns revealing something for which they were thankful. A scruffy white boy named Jeffrey declared that his family did not celebrate Thanksgiving. This was notable in and of itself, but also because he was often silent. Selena thought it might have to do with being white; perhaps he was embarrassed to talk in his squeaky voice, even though Ms. Gallagher was also white.

"That may be the case, Jeffrey," said Ms. Gallagher, "but I know there must be something you're thankful for."

"We don't celebrate Thanksgiving," Jeffrey piped up shrilly, "because it's mean. The Indians invited the Pilgrims to Thanksgiving dinner and then afterward the Pilgrims stole the Indians' tomahawks and chopped them all up. Even the children."

The class gasped. A boy named Ferrell, who occasionally got very angry and turned desks over, hooted with laughter. A gluey darkness swept over Selena.

Ms. Gallagher spoke mildly. "That's not quite correct, Jeffrey."

"But it's a little correct?" asked Lamar, who everyone agreed was the smartest in the class.

"Another story for another day," the teacher said with a slight edge. "And, Jeffrey, you don't have to tell us now, but I do want you to continue to think about what you're thankful for. That's important."

At recess, instead of playing Chinese jump rope with the girls (and Lamar), Selena sought out Jeffrey where he usually stood, alone by the dead garden, playing with a green Hess truck he'd brought for every show-and-tell since kindergarten.

"Is that true what you said?"

Jeffrey regarded her sullenly with his in-between-color eyes.

"How do you know all that stuff?" she pressed.

"Everyone knows it," he said, and walked away. She imagined kicking him in the back.

Selena didn't say anything to her parents that night, as her father chopped onions and her mother peeled sweet potatoes. Her grandmother, Aunt Braxton and Uncle Paul, Seraphim and Pater would be over. The house smelled wonderful, but in the dark at bedtime, Selena could not escape dreams about the Indians. She heard their wailing and saw the first Thanksgiving, her parents' own dining room table, white tablecloth covered in bloody handprints.

A couple of nights later, she determined to stay awake all night to avoid the nightmares. As soon as her mother had tucked her in, she padded quietly out of bed to put the light back on. One by one she drew from the stack of picture books by her bedside that she was really getting too old to read but couldn't quite leave behind. The one about the frog and the toad. The one about Frances the finicky badger. Stories about mice and rabbits. The one about the red-snowsuited little Black boy in the city in the snow . . . "he thought and thought and thought about them." When she heard her mother's step outside her door, Selena lay back and squeezed her eyes shut, dropping the book. Her mother carefully opened the door and switched off the light.

Selena lay still in the dark, refusing to close her eyes for as long as she could. And then, as if it had been waiting for her, an image of a little girl wrapped in a thin blanket popped into her head. The girl coughed, stumbled, then fell, spreading blood in the snow. Selena screamed.

"So, then what happened?" Liselle asked.

"Then they all but destroyed nearly every tribe and took their land. And in California, the Spanish made them slaves and forced them to build churches and put their bones in the buildings and—"

Liselle tried not to laugh. "No, I mean what happened to you?"

Selena turned her hands over, palms up on the table. "It's like this. That *is* what happened to me."

"What did your parents say?"

"My father lives on his own personal planet. And my mother calls it my 'worries.' It's not like I spent too much time confiding in them."

"But your mom was a school counselor, right?"

"She did have the sense to get me a therapist in high school, I guess."

"What did the therapist say?"

"She kept saying that these things weren't happening to me, and that I should focus on what was happening to me. Like when this starts happening, I should think about my body and scan all my senses." She rolled her eyes.

But in eighteenth-century Jamaica there was something called a "gibbet." What would hippie breathing exercises do about that?

Liselle was quiet for a while. "Babe, I'm sorry to be so dense, but I just don't think I get it. Like, we're here on a college campus, not on a plantation in the Caribbean."

"Maybe I shouldn't have said anything," Selena said.

It wasn't just history but also the news that plagued her. A girl had been chained up in a West Philadelphia basement; a two-year-old was raped by the highway in New York; a young Laotian boy with a bleeding bottom, trying to flee a white serial killer, was returned to the killer's home, a veritable charnel house, by Milwaukee police. He was butchered.

"That is terrible. But I still don't get what this has to do with you," Liselle said, feeling confused and inadequate.

"Look," said Selena. "Maybe it's not happening here and now, but it happened to someone. And if it happened to someone, it might as well have been me."

ne afternoon in college, when Liselle didn't answer the phone, Selena found her crying in her room.

"Tell me," said Selena, sitting down on the bed.

Liselle had gotten a B minus on an essay on *Zami* for Professor Bruin, reminding her of the old white man who'd driven her from the English Department. Obviously, this cut even closer to the bone.

"She said my paper was fantasy and not literary analysis. And that because of the socioeconomic hierarchy outlined in the book, two Black women couldn't stay together," she cried.

"Who sounds crazy now?" Selena joked. No one had said the word "crazy," Liselle thought. She'd been through a lot of Selena's moods, but she had been careful not to say "crazy." That was what you called a girl when you were done with her.

"Think about the ones in literature," Liselle said, "the girlfriends who got raped in *Brewster Place*, that one who got her hair pulled out in *Corregidora*? And then there's these women who are couples but they never hook up. Like Sula and Nel."

"Uh-huh," said Selena, who had only the slightest idea what Liselle was going on about. She had quickly given up her coveted spot in Writing a Way from No Way, and her favorite class was a first-year seminar, Self and Nature, in which she happily read Romantic poets and *Walden*.

"Well, so I was arguing that the end of *Zami* was, like, disproving this, with this character named Afrekete and—"

"Afrekete," Selena interrupted with a dreamy expression. "That's a good name."

"Just listen. They have an incredible affair, but Professor Bruin says the whole 'Afrekete' thing is an allegory for self-love, and the actual love of Audre Lorde's life was some white woman. Some old ugly white woman who never wrote anything—and anyway, she died of breast cancer two years ago!"

"The white woman?"

"No!" It was not funny to Liselle that Audre Lorde had been given to her only to be snatched away almost at the same time, but Liselle was laughing and then Selena as well.

"Promise me," Liselle said, dabbing at her eyes with a tissue.

"Anything."

"Promise me you won't wind up with some ugly white bitch."

"I promise you, Liselle, that if I wind up with some ugly white woman, I won't know she's ugly."

"You'll know she's white!"

"Anyway, I would rather fight with you than hang out with Mary Frances," Selena declared, talking about her roommate, a girl from suburban Ohio who every day discovered some new universe in staying out late, taking a sip of beer, or eating candy in bed.

"That's not saying a lot," said Liselle.

"Well, I'd rather be with you than be with my other friends."

"That's something we should talk about, Selena." Liselle laughed. "You need to make some friends."

"And you need to stop crying over a B."

"It was a B minus!"

"And to think they once called you 'the Wolf.' Look at you now."

"Hey, that's mean!" Liselle shouted. But as they ribbed each other, she suddenly felt the rightness of the world. Knowing, however, that the world was dead wrong, she knew the feeling must be Selena.

13

"Wrong address," chirped Liselle, as she walked back into the dining room.

"You should have invited them in. More the merrier," said tipsy Ron, slipping into his Philadelphia tribal accent, pronouncing "the merrier" as *da murrier*.

"My dad used to do that," said the reverend. "He would bring lost souls into our house. I remember this one squirrely dude ate dinner with us twice. I'm pretty sure he robbed our house a week later."

"I can see how you wound up in the clergy. Your father must have been very generous—and brave," said Gladys.

"Well, he kept guns in the house. And I'm pretty sure he's a congregant in my church now," Chris said.

"Your dad?" asked Winn.

"The guy who robbed our house. I just pray for him and tell the ushers to keep him away from the collection plate."

"Y'all know I live on this tiny block in Fairmount," Ivelisse said. "It's like some kind of a cult. They have T-shirts printed up and every year they have a reunion of people who used to live there. Anyway, strangers are always trying to bust into my house. Especially during the holidays. It's real crazy. Last Thanksgiving some old man was almost to the dining room before he realized he was in a room full of suspicious Puerto Ricans."

Liselle had been afraid of the woman at the door, but also sad for her. She knew she should be immune to this feeling by now, but the sight of every unhoused, insane, uncared-for Black woman chipped away at her. She both wanted to know and didn't want to know how each one got there. She found herself looking into their faces for Selena.

The last time she'd seen Selena was years ago at a big drugstore downtown. Barack Obama had just been elected for his first term, and the Black city was full of itself. Every other person was wearing a cheap T-shirt bearing his face or slogan, jackets open on the brisk day to show them off. It was a revolution of beautiful tastelessness. Liselle smiled at strangers and nodded. As she strolled the store aisles, Liselle could hear the cashiers. "I still can't believe it," one of them said. "I waited three hours to vote. I'm usually out of there in ten minutes."

Liselle had dreamed about Obama almost every night for weeks. In one dream, they walked on the beach together, leaving only one set of footprints. In another, he offered to cut Patrice's hair and invited Liselle to sleep with him, his wife, *and* his wife's mother. In waking life, Liselle had been nervous in the voting booth, so keyed up with hope she worried she'd have some kind of seizure and vote for the Green Party.

She knew there was only so much he could do for them, and that maybe he'd be killed. The white people frothed with rage, potentially enough to stoke the poorly banked embers of the Civil War. And, political genius or not, what could he ever do about the rising water and burning air? Half of America didn't even believe in it.

Still, the day after the election, Liselle floated around the drugstore. "Yes, we can," he had repeated, his clipped speech quasi-musical

in its lack of music. Then she saw Selena at the other end of the oral
care aisle, studying the brands of toothpaste.

Even from a distance she looked bleary-eyed and behind the beat.
As Liselle approached she took in Selena's fuzzy hair, gray sweat-
pants, and dull eyes. She had a quick image of putting her in a hot
bath, scrubbing away the years, burnishing her back to a shine.

Liselle said her name.

Selena looked up from the box in her hand. "Oh, hey," she said,
as if they had come downtown together to run errands and gotten
separated.

"What are you up to?" asked Liselle.

"Readjusting to civilian life."

"Civilian—?"

"I was in the hospital."

Liselle had found out from the alumnae rumor mill about the
first time Selena had been in the psych ward, but that was almost
fifteen years ago. So this would be at least the second time. She nodded, then followed Selena's eyes down to her left hand, to Winn's
great-grandmother's engagement diamond, placed in a new setting.

"I got married," said Liselle, sheepish.

Selena's mouth smiled. "Evidently."

"You don't know this per—"

"Him."

"Right. You don't know him."

"Of course not. Do you all have children?"

"I have a boy," said Liselle. "His name is Patrice."

"You're a mom," said Selena. "Wow."

"Well," said Liselle, trying to smile. Feeling uncomfortable as this
particular woman called her a mom, she thought to change the subject and simply said, "Obama."

"Yes, Obama won, and you are married with a kid. Time is a busy motherfucker." Both Selena's voice and expression remained bland. With a lethargic movement, she lifted a shopping basket containing only vitamins. "Well, I better finish up here . . ."

Liselle, with tears in her throat, meant only to touch Selena's arm, but pulled her thin, stiff body into a hug. She smelled like hair grease and dryer sheets. "It's okay," Selena said, muffled by Liselle's shoulder. "It's hard now, but I'll be okay." She pulled herself away.

Liselle stood in the aisle wiping away tears as varieties of floss blurred before her eyes. An older white woman in a store apron with a kind face was offering her a tissue and saying something about Obama. When Liselle finally made her way to the front of the store, she was sure she saw Selena's shopping basket abandoned in front of a magazine display.

14

early four months into their affair, Liselle looked out her dorm room window into the frozen skies and thought it was suddenly too much.

"What," Selena said in a nasty voice, "are you looking at?"

"Just taking a break from defending myself."

"Do you think disappearing for two days is okay? Look, you're the first woman I've ever been with. Do you think there's any responsibility in that?"

"I *didn't* disappear. This campus is the size of a bath mat. And anyway, I may be your first *woman*, Selena, but you know how to handle yourself. I'm not your *first*—not by a long shot."

"Don't you bring that up! That's fucking low. Anyway, as fucked-up as it is, you're just jealous that you couldn't catch a dick if you were hanging out in a urinal."

Less than twenty-four hours before this, during another fight, Liselle had given a speech about how they were not fighting each other, but fighting through something to make it better. It had seemed like the right thing to say at the time. Now she felt it was important to say, "This is bullshit."

"I totally fucking agree on all counts," said Selena. "But it's bullshit *you* pulled me into. I just got here. I didn't know anything and then I wound up here, with *you*."

"Oh, is that your story now? Are you one of these little innocent white girls?"

"Those white girls are wrong about most things, but they were right about *you*."

Before she'd thought about it, Liselle had grabbed Selena and was pushing her against the heating unit by the window. With one hand she held Selena; with the other she was untwisting the window's handle to throw her out of it. Selena suddenly became very strong and pushed Liselle across the room, knocking her into the cheap particleboard dresser. Liselle slumped to the floor, catching her breath.

"I should have let you do it," said Selena in a low voice. "It would have been my pleasure. It would have been the best day of my fucking life."

"Selena! Are you okay in there?" Liselle recognized the voice of the resident assistant.

"I'm fine, Jill," Selena called out in a flat voice, as she looked into Liselle's imploring eyes. "I just tripped."

Later that day they had marathon sex. Intermittently, Liselle cried and apologized. Selena dried her tears with kisses. Liselle had a shuddering orgasm that she remembered years later.

15

It was over by the time the campus broke for winter vacation. Each remembered the end differently.

Selena always remembered that Liselle, walking with a group of other girls, did not speak to her as they passed each other on the icy path to the library.

Liselle remembered that Selena had come into the cafeteria, looked at her, and walked right back out.

16

Girl!" Vanessa was exclaiming as she speared the chicken in the fig sauce. "I have got to get this recipe from you." Liselle smiled distantly. Vanessa had asked for the recipe no fewer than three times, and each time Liselle had told her that it had been catered by Linda & Sons and wasn't hers to give. Liselle suspected that when Vanessa remembered conversations, she remembered only her own side of them.

"It is quite delicious," said Gladys. But though they'd been at many tables together over the years, Liselle wasn't sure she'd seen Gladys put food in her mouth. She was seventy-five but looked near ninety. On the tall side, even stooped with age, she weighed perhaps one hundred pounds soaking wet. Her expensive-looking wool suit draped her like a bathrobe. Looking at her made Liselle feel like a hippopotamus. She had to remind herself she was merely normal-sized for a Black woman in Philadelphia, and since she definitely wasn't going to be Michelle Obama she could stop drinking hot lemon water for lunch, pinching her middle, and wondering if she was good enough.

"I'm glad you like it, Gladys," said Liselle. She tried not to look at the woman's claw, its startling bluish veins. But then her face, its Virginia Woolf hollows, struck Liselle as poignant, though it was emotionally wasteful to feel sorry for rich white women. They made their choices. Or did they? She could hear Gladys's voice in her head asking, *Who would willingly starve half to death?* Then she heard Gladys's actual voice.

"When can I have a word with you and Winn? I don't like to drive home too late."

"Did you drive?" Liselle asked. "I thought we agreed you were going to take a cab."

"Cabs are so expensive. Speaking of that—"

Someone at the other end of the table was hitting a glass with a fork as if they were in a massive banquet hall. Ron Mack stood.

"What are you doing, bud?" Winn asked. "Sit down."

"I will not sit. I will propose a toast," he announced. Liselle saw Ivelisse looking at him appreciatively. Ivelisse, she knew, had a thing for mediocre white men. That "all-American thing," she'd said once.

"Oh God," said Winn. "Let's save the emoting for dessert, please." But Liselle could see he was thrilled to be toasted.

(*Fix your face*, said Verity.)

"This man," Ron started. "Well, first, let's get this elephant out here in the open and send him packing. We lost."

"Awwww!" yelled Vanessa. Ivelisse smiled sadly. Liza and Gary Appleton regarded Liselle with frank curiosity. She tried to communicate her distaste for Ron to them, even as she fixed her face.

"You lost, my man. This dusty old establishment wasn't ready for a change!"

"Boo!" Vanessa yelled.

"Hiss!" chimed Ivelisse.

"That goddamned Church Williams," hissed Liza.

"His real name is Parnell," Chris said.

Ron continued, "But you're not the only one who lost. The people of Philadelphia missed out on a chance at some fresh, smart energy. But there was also some winning—"

"Winning!" shouted Winn.

"You got much further in this district than some white real estate lawyer from Connecticut was supposed to."

Yeah, I said it, he seemed to say with a pause. White people rarely said "white" in mixed company unless they were making a cluelessly racist joke about how "white" they were. Liselle looked at Chris, whose expression made her imagine him listening to the confidences of a particularly amoral congregant.

"You won our attention and loyalty beyond what friendship has engendered. And I'm telling you, brother, you will have that, the attention and loyalty, for as long as you—"

"Hear! Hear!" said Gladys Banfield, surprisingly loud, cutting him off.

Liselle raised her glass.

As Winn rose, he and Ron gripped each other dramatically. Gladys hissed into Liselle's ear, "I despise that man. Itsy would have hated him." Itsy was her name for Winn's mother.

"Speech!" said Ivelisse.

Winn stood, smiling, and put his hand on his heart. He was flushed with the night and with drink.

"Ivelisse," he said. She bowed her head humbly. "Ron, Vanessa . . . *Chris.*" He sighed, though Chris looked bored. He reeled off the remaining names, causing Liselle to wonder if he'd given any thought to the order. "We certainly don't have time right now for me to say what I actually need to say to you all."

Dizzy with alienation, and though they were down to an oversweet Malbec, Liselle poured a glass of wine so heavy her wrist strained to pick it up. It had been smart of her to send Patrice away. She thought of a song he liked; he would bark, "Leaviton!" when it came on in the car, a singsongy new rap song. *Started from the bottom, now we here / Started from the bottom, now the whole team [scratch] here.* What was the opposite of that lyric? She thought of herself earlier on the phone talking to the FBI, then saying "Afrekete" to Selena's mother, and wanted to crawl under the table for having done something so odd, sentimental, and desperate; she should have been assembling the family's passports and investigating extradition treaties.

Winn was doing a thing he sometimes did—no one told him to do it, certainly not Ivelisse, who had gone over all of his speeches with him—where he imitated the president, the way he clipped some of his words, the pauses he added, the way he said "future." It was slight; no one would notice but Liselle. He wound up his inelegant series of thank-yous: "I don't know [*Obama pause*] what my future holds [*pause*] but I do know [*pause*] I want to see all of you in it."

As if she'd been waiting in the kitchen for him to finish, Xochitl came gliding into the room. Liselle noted that though Winn had shouted out the caterers who were not there, he had not mentioned Xochitl, who was present, nor the absent Jimena, who had heated up hundreds of puff pastries and assembled countless to-go containers. Once, a guest—they never knew who—had become very ill in the bathroom. Over Liselle's (admittedly weak) protests, Jimena had insisted on handling that as well.

As Xochitl poured coffee, Liselle went to get a large glass bowl of bourbon-spiked whipped cream and a plum tart that she knew the men would maul and the women would try to ignore. When she came back and set it on the table, she could feel Xochitl regarding her with disapproval. Liselle ignored her and continued to clear.

When Liselle brought the last dinner fork into the kitchen, Xochitl stood at the sink, staring out into the yard, chewing on her hair. Liselle stood next to her, thinking of a storm last summer. Winn had been off meeting with people who could do something for the election, perhaps sealing his fate as a criminal. Liselle had been looking for a blouse in the attic when the rain started to fall, thumping and splattering the house with rage. The thunder, which exploded shortly after, seemed beside the point. She had come down from the third floor, her heart beating rapidly. The rain had sounded out of control, like a storm she'd witnessed once on a trip with Verity to Barbados. One moment they'd been in the marketplace under sunshine so hard it felt rhythmic, and then the sky had opened up and the rain had battered their skin all the way back to the hotel.

Prowling around the house, she had tried to get away from the sound of Caribbean rain in Philadelphia. Walking by his room, she had been surprised to find Patrice home rather than looking at comic books at Big Blue Marble, where he spent most summer afternoons. She could see his filthy sneakers, unlawfully propped up on the edge of his bed, through a wide crack in his door. She pushed in and found him sleeping, with his hands folded on his chest, a manga facedown on his stomach; all he read were manga. Liselle worried about his brain, but his unibrow looked peaceful. She stood in the doorway, watching him until she began to feel sleepy. The rain continued, so she sat at the edge of his bed and tried to match her breathing to his. He woke to find her sitting there.

"Visiting hours?" he said.

"I was just—" she said. "That's a lot of rain."

"Is it a hurricane?" he asked sleepily. Once, at age four, he had gotten Winn to operate the video camera while he made a movie of himself acting out different types of natural disasters. Liselle had been in charge of helping him with the wardrobe. He had movements and outfits for each disaster. He named them after himself: Hurricane Patrice. Tornado Patrice. Tropical Depression Patrice. She and Winn had watched the video over and over again, impressed with the fact that their smart, eccentric son seemed more interested by than afraid of disaster.

"I guess it's just a thunderstorm," she said.

"Tropical Depression Liselle," he said.

Liselle wondered what Patrice would think of Selena and her

obsession with past and impending horrors. (What Liselle did not know: Selena had been at a bus stop in the rainstorm, headed home from the bakery. Unlike the squealing people crowding the shelter, Selena had stood calmly, allowing the rain to blow in and pelt her arms and legs. She had been reading for some time about storms and the earth. The north was becoming the south, the south becoming hell. The end of this world was not a delusion but an imminent fact. A calm settled over her body at this thought. She longed for someone to tell; her mind surprised her by landing on Liselle.)

In her kitchen, Liselle remembered that she'd been meaning to replace the motion sensor light in the yard. The bulb had died weeks ago and nighttime was too dark out there for weeks. The bushes made threatening shapes. Was there a van full of surveillance equipment in the shadows listening to everything she and Winn said and did?

"Xochitl," Liselle said, concentrating on pronunciation, "you can go home."

"Are you sure?" Xochitl said. Together they surveyed the kitchen, which looked like the battlefield after a catered war. "I mean, I could always use the money in staying, but to be honest, the time is more important. My diss prospectus is due in two weeks."

What the hell was a "diss prospectus"? Liselle said, "I'll pay you what I would have if you stayed through cleanup. Anyway, I have plenty of help. Patrice will be home later tonight." As she spoke she knew it was true. She was going to bring Patrice home, even if she had to wake him up at Adam's, even if she had to wake up Miriam Blau to wake up Adam to wake up Patrice. She wanted him close.

"How *is* Patrice?" asked Gladys, suddenly crowding the kitchen. Her violently shaking hand weaponized a bone china mug of hot decaf. Liselle backed away, wondering if Gladys actually meant to threaten her with the coffee.

"Can I get you something?"

"In a manner of speaking," said Gladys. Turning to Xochitl she said, "Miss, may I have a word with your employer?"

Liselle cleared her throat as if to excuse Gladys. "I'm sorry, Xochitl. Maybe head into the sitting room and take a break? Just for a moment."

"But, Ms. Belmont, there's so much to do; I don't want anyone to think I'm just . . ."

"I want my money back!" Gladys yelled. Xochitl sprinted out of the kitchen.

"Look, I don't mean to yell," said Gladys, "but I haven't been able to get Winn on the phone for weeks and I can't wait another minute to talk about this. I'm generous, Freddie always said so, but I have my limits."

Up until then there had been a hum of voices in the dining room. Now Liselle heard only an upbeat tune by the Brand New Heavies, which reminded her viscerally of a club in New York in the nineties. Wetlands.

"Gladys," she said in a deceptively calm voice. "What are you talking about?"

"The money I loaned to the campaign? When will I get it back?"

"Those were donations," said Liselle. But she didn't really know what to say, because as she had recently learned, she did not know anything about anything.

"No one made that clear to me. And where does that money go, anyway, when you lose?"

Ron came into the kitchen, Winn on his heels.

"What's wrong, Aunt Gladys?" Winn asked, though Liselle knew he had heard.

Gladys's eyes looked purple. "It's getting late. I just wanted to inquire about the status of my money before I left this house tonight. I'm not a pushover like your mother, God rest her soul. You know that, Winnie."

Liselle didn't know if Winn's ashen expression was a response to the mention of the money or his mother. He opened his mouth but nothing came out.

"I think this is something I can help with," said Ron.

"Well, I don't know why that would be," said Gladys, who gave the impression of looking down on Ron, who stood about a head taller than she did.

Liselle felt curious about what would happen next, but Winn touched her lower back. "Honey"—honey!—"why don't you go check on our guests?"

"Maybe I can just write you a check for now," she heard Ron say, as she drifted back into the dining room. But then who would pay that back? She looked at Winn, whose panicked expression made her feel unsteady. He thought *this* was a problem? She wanted to laugh. It struck her that no one would ever claim Winn was their rock. Who was the rock? Didn't every family, every person, have one?

◎◎ **17** ◎◎

The girl Liselle dated after Selena literally paled in comparison. Garcia was a sophomore who looked like a brunette Marcia Brady, but her weedy smell and spacey ways recalled her namesake, Jerry. Liselle needed something to distract her from grief and regret. In the meantime, Selena could be seen around campus, looking oddly pale, sometimes with Mary Frances, but mainly alone. Liselle could not be sure but she thought Selena might be talking to herself.

One night in her final semester of college, Liselle sat in the stacks reading Henry Louis Gates and listening to Tupac, hoping her thesis, an excavation of hip-hop lyrics, would emerge fully formed from her brain. Across from her, Garcia was asleep, catching flies with her mouth. That was a thing to be learned from white girls. She and Garcia had been dating only a couple of weeks, but even if they stayed together for twenty years, Liselle felt she would not fall asleep in front of her in public under fluorescent lights. Riveted by the sight of freedom, Liselle did not hear anyone approaching. She jumped at the sensation of a hand on her shoulder.

"Hi," said Selena. Her eyes seemed larger, but eyes didn't get bigger; she was thinner. Her exposed collarbones looked sharp. Her lips were badly chapped. It was late March, cold and wet, the despised yearly spring fake-out.

"Hi, Selena."

"This your girlfriend," Selena said, no question mark.

"Well," Liselle began, "I mean—"

"I know I asked, but I don't care."

Liselle waited.

Selena said, "Did you know there's nothing at all about the MOVE fire in this whole library?"

"What?"

"There's nothing about the MOVE bombing in this library," Selena repeated.

"Are you doing research about MOVE? For what class?"

"What does it matter? I just think that's fucked. We're *in* Philadelphia—"

"Well, technically—"

"We're not even *across a river* from Philadelphia. This was, what, ten years ago? Why is there no sign of it in the library?"

"Did you look in the newspaper microfilms?"

"Hey," said Garcia, suddenly awake, looking at Selena. "Aren't you in my Eastern Religions class?"

Selena looked at Garcia, who was smiling for some reason. "No, Liselle, it isn't in the microfilms. Obviously the first place I'd look is the microfilms. For some reason all those microfilms are gone. And I'm not in your Eastern Religions class. I would never take that bullshit. Everybody knows the professor goes to Thailand every year to sleep with teenage prostitutes." She turned and left.

Garcia said, "I really think she's in my class."

Liselle sighed, needing silence, but it was not to be. Garcia held forth on Selena's dark energy, as well as on how it was wrong to assume sex workers didn't have as much autonomy and agency as the American women who wore disfiguring shoes to corporate jobs every day.

"Maybe *they* should be thought of as prostitutes," she said passionately. Liselle broke up with her shortly after.

As her college career wound down, the days became a whirlwind of last this, last that. At the end of each one, Liselle collapsed and slept like the dead. But one afternoon, when she was supposed to be looking for something else entirely, she found herself scrolling through the spring 1985 *Philadelphia Inquirer* microfilm. The MOVE story was right where the catalog said it should be.

Her stomach churned as she looked at aerial views of the smoldering rows (and rows) of homes; the small scarecrow of a boy in the arms of a police officer; the short woman with a neck-straining head of hair who had escaped, her eyes both blank and fathomless, reminding Liselle of the last time she'd seen Selena.

"There's nothing about the MOVE bombing in this library"; it was not a fact but some kind of message. What was the message?

Liselle shut down the machine and put the microfilm box on the return cart.

On graduation day, most of underclassmen had left campus for the summer. As Liselle walked carefully across the stage in the new Doc Martens that Verity had not wanted her to wear in the shimmering June heat, she saw something by the trees, a gaunt, dark shadow in a yellow dress. Liselle wiped the sweat out of her eyes and shook the firm, dry hand of the president. When she looked back at the trees, Selena was gone.

18

After graduation Liselle achieved the widespread generic dream of winding up in New York. Like many of the dreamers, she found cramped, expensive living quarters, sharing an apartment that straddled the Upper East Side and East Harlem. She had found her three roommates through a Bryn Mawr message board.

She spent her workdays in a cubicle surrounded by other cubicles full of young people, mostly white, at a startup called Media Inc. Her near neighbor Luther was cigar-colored and claimed *Spain*-Spanish roots, though his full name was Lutherio and his family lived in Washington Heights. There was also Sasha, who'd graduated from the University of Vermont, and Winn, who'd gone to NYU to escape Connecticut.

They worked in a Midtown office building temporally located somewhere between the dying industry of magazines and the frontier of the World Wide Web. Their boss, an excitable nephew of some bigwig at Hearst, their parent company, was prone to saying, "No one knows how far this thing is gonna go."

Luther, Sasha, Winn, and Liselle had the job of dumping magazine recipes online. Talking about work was prohibitively boring; at lunch they played Fuck, Marry, Kill.

"Fuck Michael, kill Madonna, marry Prince," said Sasha, who often pulled her sleeves over her hands as if she were enjoying a catalog weekend in a country cabin. It was the mid-nineties and the cultural imagination had not changed its calendar page from eighties celebrities.

"You would have sex with Michael Jackson?" gasped Liselle.

"Well, I can't marry him," whined Sasha. "Then I'd be stuck in that castle forever."

"No woman is allowed to stay there past the prenuptial statutes," said Winn, sipping white wine. If they went anywhere better than a sandwich shop for lunch, Winn always had a glass or two. Liselle did not understand how he could work after that, but he never seemed affected and chalked it up to his "*Mayflower* constitution."

"You could have sex with that . . . ? His bleached hands? His Jheri curl?" Liselle wondered if white people understood Jheri curls; if they could identify the cloying smell of curl activator that she had learned about during Verity's brief phase. "What do you think he would say to you while you were doing it?"

Sasha squeezed her eyes shut. "I hope nothing. What about you, Winn? What would you do?"

"Marry Michael Jackson for his money," he said. "Fuck Madonna *and* Prince. Best threesome ever." Before Winn, Liselle had only read about twinkling eyes. It wasn't cute, she thought. Let no one accuse her of thinking it was cute.

"That's faggot shit, man," said Luther.

Liselle rolled her eyes and Sasha laughed nervously, pulling at her distended sweater sleeve. This was Luther's role in their foursome, being Homeboy from the Streets. This, despite the fact that he'd gone to some college in upstate New York with a ski team. He was complicated like a fancy French dessert. Years later, Liselle would learn that he had spent several months, while they'd known him, being "kept" in a Tribeca apartment by one of the married

EVPs at the company. That was the first time she'd ever heard of a woman running game like that.

"Luther, you're so homophobic," said Sasha. Liselle knew that, strictly speaking, this was her line, considering she was the only out gay person at the table. But she just listened.

"It's no fear," he said. "'Phobic' means 'fear.' I am not afraid. I'm stating a true fact. This is literally gay shit."

Winn shrugged. "And I'm just playing the game. What would you do, Luther? Mow them all down with a semiautomatic like Scarface?"

Liselle laughed. "Luther, you never answer the question. Answer the question."

"It's not fun, Luther," said Sasha.

Luther sucked his teeth. "We always up here talking about what celebrities we would fuck and who we would eat if we got trapped in the office. Shit's childish. Look at those guys over there," he said, gesturing to some fat, white, suited types. "They're talking about how to take over the world."

Winn smirked. "Well, there's three of them, Luther. It's perfect. Fuck, marry, kill?" Lunch break was winding down. This was one of those times they'd have to run, like when they'd waited forty-five minutes at the famous soup stand. The longer they'd waited, the more no one wanted to have wasted their time. Finally, almost late for an editorial meeting, they dashed across crowded avenues carrying containers of scalding liquid. Poor Sasha tripped just outside of the building, spattering her clothes with zucchini cream, which of course looked like vomit. (*Pobrecita*, said Luther, but he was laughing.)

"All right," Luther said, reclining away from the table, with a curl to his lips. As he spoke he looked at (1) Liselle, (2) Sasha, and (3) Winn. "Well, I would fuck *you*, marry you, and kill you, obviously." He added, "No offense, man."

"None taken," said Winn. Sasha's cheeks rashed red, which disgusted Liselle, who had a pet peeve about blushing. As for herself, Liselle felt light-headed, because as generally unappealing as he was, Luther had looked at her and said *fuck*.

Liselle had been more or less celibate since she'd graduated and moved from the campus. She'd had a couple of uninspired hookups, including one when a demonstrably acrobatic Black woman from London had spent the night and Liselle woke up to find her rifling through her purse. She knew there must be friendly and available lesbians somewhere in the city of New York. So far, though, she had seen mostly glamorous, scary ones: all colors of brown with glistening cornrows, in huge puffy jackets and tan Timberland boots, striding through subway stations like Naomi Campbell, or white and angular, their haircuts sharp enough to slice meat. Liselle felt muffled and angry, rubbing herself raw at night while her roommates banged about in the cluttered, thin-walled apartment. She felt as if a chartered church bus had left her stranded in the city.

Still, New York turned her on—not just the unattainable women, but the broad, sparkling avenues of Midtown, the shimmering blouses in Fifth Avenue shopwindows, the thick paint smell of art galleries, the end-of-this-world wrongness of the lights in Times Square, crowded uptown movie theaters full of Black people laughing at the violent parts. She was titillated by the teenagers making out passionately on the train and the fact that she could buy Chinese soup dumplings at three o'clock in the morning.

Though her roommates were nice enough, she barely had any friends, and she was not having enough sex or any. It was beginning to make her weird enough to think, *Well, maybe Luther*, even if he was a man, and also one of those people who got less attractive the more they spoke. She was not, at that time, paying attention to Winn. And in any case, she assumed he was gay, or if not that, she wondered if he had some kind of debauched and confusing rich white-person sexuality, as in the Whit Stillman movies beloved by one of the unsubstantial girls she'd dated after Selena.

At one of the meetings, the site editors discussed a calendar of holiday themes for the pages. The boss could scarcely contain himself at the possibilities. "Thanksgiving!" he roared. "Valentine's!" There were hundreds of pages of old recipes and lifestyle tips in the Hearst archives that they could revive with links. The editorial assistants furiously scribbled notes.

When someone said Saint Patrick's Day, Winn snorted with laughter but the room was quiet.

"What's so funny, Winnifred?" asked the boss.

Winn, the only one of them who had earned a funny nickname, shrugged. "What are we going to do on the site for Saint Patrick's Day? Oppose busing?" Liselle had been sipping water and choked with laughter.

"You're a piece of work, buddy," the boss said fondly, a tone he reserved for the men in the office. This was exasperating; still, Liselle continued to laugh at Winn's joke for years, long after she knew Winn had forgotten it. This would have been the moment she and Winn caught each other's eye across the crowded room in the movie version of their courtship that would never be made.

fter two years in New York, Liselle moved back to Philadelphia. She had been toying with the idea of leaving her job for about a year before she did it, around the time that Winn announced he was leaving for law school and Luther began hinting that he knew that mass layoffs were coming to Media. While Liselle couldn't envision something like a career, she came across a listing for a middle school history teaching position at Quaker Academy. She rightly presumed they needed Black teachers and knew they did not require certification.

After a few suffocating months in Verity's house listening to her signify about having to pay off tuition loans, Liselle overdrew her account to make a deposit on a small apartment in Mt. Airy. Her new job was fine, but not especially rewarding. She cared little for Quaker Academy's middle-class/wealthy students, mostly white, some Black or Asian (there were no Latinos). She didn't see herself in them. Of the four jobs she'd interviewed for when she got back to Philadelphia—one at an education nonprofit, another at a medical publisher, and one as a paralegal—it was the only one she got.

Compared with where she'd grown up, in West Philly, the

Northwest was exotic, with its integrated hippie scene and boxy, old white lesbians. Sometimes on her bus ride to work, she remembered talking with Selena about what they wanted to be; Selena had wanted only "to help women." During college and sometimes after, Liselle told people she wanted to become a writer like her fellow anthropology student Zora Neale Hurston. But sometimes she lay alone in her room listening to music and imagined herself behind the boards at a dance club—a DJ. This dream, she knew, was going nowhere. She had a better chance of being a writer in the Harlem Renaissance.

For companionship, she occasionally went for beers with the woodshop teacher, a salty, old-fashioned dyke who'd had the same girlfriend for fifteen years. For love or whatever, she had a thing going with a very pierced Black woman who worked at Weavers Way. Fall turned into winter and the days were pewter-colored. She could support herself and chip away at her loans; that was good, she thought, as she passed soiled and raving Black women on the street in Center City. But she was bored by her job and only somewhat less lonely with her unserious girlfriend, who chattered on about her food allergies and previous lives. Liselle wondered where her current life was going.

Then came two surprises.

The first was an email from an unrecognizable address with the subject line "Baby Girl."

"I'm ignoring it," she told Verity in the cafeteria at IKEA, where they had come to shop for plastic bins, curtains, and a bath mat for Liselle's new place.

Verity moved her shoulders up and down in a deliberate and artificial motion; she was not the shrugging kind. "Your father; your life. Do whatever you want."

"Like I said, I'm ignoring it."

"And *I* said do whatever you want with that faggot."

Liselle stared. The meatball went dry in her mouth. "Are you saying my father is gay?"

Nearby, a young white couple with a placid baby in a high chair looked over furtively.

"You didn't hear me say anything about gay. I said he was a *faggot*"—the couple winced—"who left his wife and three-year-old daughter so he could go to California and wear shorts every day."

"You can't keep saying that word," snapped Liselle. The couple began hurriedly packing their things. The baby squalled angrily and grabbed for crackers.

Verity looked at her. "O-kay," she said, patting Liselle's thigh twice in time. Liselle remembered once when Verity had slapped her. She did not remember exactly what had happened, but had the feeling she'd asked a question about her father, whom, of course, she was going to meet.

Dark fell fast on the October afternoon when Liselle found herself waiting in the bakery near the school where she worked. It was a warm, bright place where all the pastries tasted like sweet cardboard. She sipped coffee that she drank for courage, though she knew it would keep her up into the night stewing over whatever happened here today.

Despite the intervening years, her father was instantly recognizable from the sole photo of him that Verity had let her keep. She had studied the picture; he leaned on a black Porsche in an open-necked dress shirt. As in the photo, the details of his appearance created a visual symphony called "well cared for." It took a lot of up-close concentration to note the deep crease in his forehead, and the fact that his hair was a shade too black, shoe polish–like.

"I can't believe it," he said with a smile, his eyes growing dewy. One of the things she knew about him from Verity was that he liked to drive the car with the top down, even when it had been chilly. Long after he'd left, as they watched *Waiting to Exhale*, Verity had screamed "Get the car!" at Angela Bassett as she destroyed her cheating husband's things.

Without looking, Liselle knew that women in the café were staring. She let herself be hugged, feeling smug and then foolish.

Her father drank hot water, saying it was something he'd learned from his girlfriend of three years. Ann was Korean American and only slightly older than Liselle. "Wise for her age," he said. These were nervous digressions; he clearly hadn't meant to tell Liselle that he was dating someone her age. Then he got to the point. What had finally "lit a fire under his ass" to "reconnect" with Liselle was that Ann was pregnant, and he needed to think seriously about family. Then he tried to explain why he'd disappeared all those years ago.

"Look, Liselle, I just got . . . distracted."

"Distracted," Liselle repeated. She thought about an episode of *The Oprah Winfrey Show* she'd watched with Selena. There had been a long video montage buildup to a father-child reunion. Finally, the father was sitting next to his daughter onstage, her eyes glistening. He turned and faced her (and Oprah), ready to explain what had happened. "Basically," he started, and Liselle had started laughing; neither she nor Selena heard the rest of what he said. After fifteen years in the wind this asshole began his answer with "basically."

Now her own father explained, "There were so many times I almost hopped on a flight here. Many times I picked up the phone to call. Once, Ann can confirm this, we were in DC and I went right up to the Amtrak kiosk; I was on a mission to get a ticket to Philly. That was two years ago. But the longer things went, it just . . ."

"Went longer?" said Liselle.

"Your mother's daughter," he said with a little smile. "I know it doesn't sound right. But I'm just being honest. First it was one thing, then another, then another. Then I convinced myself that you wouldn't see me, or that Verity wouldn't let me see you. I just couldn't get my shit together. By the way, do you remember the Porsche?"

She nodded. *I remember it as much as I remember you. Maybe the Porsche is my real father.*

"I was so unhappy here in Philly. Everything was so gray and sad and segregated. Things just didn't seem possible. And your mother would not even entertain the idea of a move out of West Philly, let alone anywhere new. You know how she just says no with her whole self? I know I shouldn't speak badly of her and I'm not trying to; I can tell she was a great mom. So even though I loved you more than anything, I got it in my mind that if I could drive it out to the West Coast with the top off, in the sun, then I would be happy." He emitted a harsh little laugh. "I grant you that I had kind of lost my mind."

"Okay," Liselle said.

Liselle was aware that her father, when he'd disappeared in his stupid car, had been about her age. The words he'd used: "gray and sad and segregated"—she felt them develop into a lump in her throat.

She swallowed. "Did it work? Did you feel better when you got there?"

"Well, the car died in Phoenix, near the desert. It was a beautiful piece of junk I had bought from my uncle when he went to prison. But your mother wired me the money to take a train to LA. And after a while, I did feel better, I guess. I broke into film, doing sound, as you probably heard from you mom."

She hadn't.

"Well, have you ever seen the movie *Cocktail?*"

She looked at him.

"I missed you both. I truly did. But I knew I couldn't breathe here, and that if I stayed, we might all wind up on the news."

Liselle thought about that for a moment. "Can I ask—is all of this an elaborate way of telling me you're gay? Because, like, I don't care. I'm—"

"Ah, Verity. I guess she told you that." He laughed. "That's fair.

I was trying a lot of things out then. But I'm with Ann now, and, frankly, sexuality was the least of it."

"What was the most of it?"

He laughed again. He laughed a lot.

"Well, back when I was in Philly, I did sound work for concerts, so I was around a lot of musicians. They are surprisingly generous with their drugs. Luckily, I decided early on that wasn't my scene. But I'm not really gay. I mean, everybody's a little bit gay, right?" (He laughed.)

Before Liselle could affirm that, he put down his mug and clapped.

"Okay, that's me for now, but I want to hear about you. Tell me everything," he said. "Let's start today and move backward."

Liselle had an unpleasant sense of déjà vu. She saw herself in Greenwich Village at a coffee shop sitting across from a skinny, bug-eyed white woman who could not stop talking: her first internet date. In a sense this was her second. She wondered what it would mean to have a father. The street was almost completely dark through the bakery windows; she heard cars laboring over the cobblestones. But in her mind she saw a sunny beach, a door open to an airy bungalow like the one on *Three's Company*; his home was a new place to go in her mind.

20

Sometime that winter, after Liselle's reunion with her father, Riva broke up with her to join a yoga cult in upstate New York, and the friendly lesbian at Quaker Academy effectively ended their friendship by reminiscing fondly about the Rizzo era one night at the pool hall. Liselle had not heard from her father since he'd returned to California. As an experiment, she sent him a long email detailing her romantic and professional mishaps. She peppered the message with questions about his life. Did he believe in God?

Days ticked by with no response. Then months. *Don't tell Verity*, she thought. *Don't tell Verity*. But Verity knew; Liselle could tell by the way she didn't ask.

Liselle taught her classes, journaled about her unhappiness, patiently waited for an appointment with a new therapist, but found herself one evening, phone in hand, tentatively punching her father's numbers. His voice when he answered was weary and hostile. "Who?"

"Ann lost the baby," he said when he finally understood who she was. Liselle apologized profusely for calling and for the miscarriage.

"It's not your fault," he said. "I'll call you soon, okay?" Liselle could hear a woman's voice in the background. She couldn't hear words, just the irritable, questioning tone.

It was almost spring by the time Liselle finally broke down and told Verity, who listened without saying anything shitty. By then she understood that she'd likely never see or speak to her father again. He had, in fact, gone back to not being her father at all. And it was then, as if taking his turn on an episode of *This Is Your Life*, that Winn reappeared.

"Talk about Philadelphia?" said his email subject line. He was coming there to do job interviews and wanted to meet up with her. Still feeling bitter about what had gone down when her father (that fucking sperm donor) contacted her out of the blue, she leaned toward not seeing Winn. It would have been more meaningful if it had been Luther, to whom Liselle, in retrospect, found herself frankly attracted, or even Sasha, who was at least a woman. And no matter who came to town, making plans with people who had suddenly stepped off planes and trains was a sad, secondhand way of living.

Still the gray of some mornings brought not full-fledged *suicidal ideations*, but questions. She thought of how, when they'd been together, Selena had been the sad one and it had boosted Liselle. But now she wanted to ask her: *Is it better to be alive than it is to be a stone? Is it better to be dead than go to work on a rainy morning?* To go out with Winn or not to be, that was the question.

On a windy April evening, after an awkward hug, she and Winn faced each other in a vinyl booth in the hipster diner on Spring Garden Street. He rattled on about Fordham Law School, his alma mater, how underrated it was, and on to the unbelievably cheap housing prices in Philadelphia. He said the place where he'd interviewed was almost as good as any of the ones in New York where he'd applied. He made sure she knew that they had reached out to recruit *him*.

Liselle's eyes must have revealed the boredom she felt, because he suddenly looked apologetic. "Let me shut the fuck up," he said. "What's been happening with you?" He ran a hand through his hair, reminding her generally of the Brat Pack and of a couple of the girls she'd been with in college.

"I teach middle school history," she said, tasting dust in her mouth. She thought about the gleaming historical building, her earnest white students, who were mostly only a little racist, and the casual snobbery of the faculty—especially the two other Black teachers.

"That what you want to be doing?" he asked, his eyes flickering between french fries and her face.

She froze. No one had asked her that in a long time. She was too embarrassed to tell him the old cover story that she wanted to be a writer, or of her ridiculous fantasies of being a DJ, of melting "Once in a Lifetime" by Talking Heads into "It's Alright" by Jay-Z, the crowd erupting in ecstasy.

"I guess it's fine," she said finally. "Did you always want to be a lawyer?" she asked him. "I feel like back at Media Inc., you once said you wanted to write plays."

"I still do. I'll be the John Grisham of the theater with a focus on Pennsylvania real estate law."

"A virtuoso of entirely empty auditoriums," Liselle said.

Winn's face turned serious. "They better offer me this job. This is civilized society's last chance at me."

"Meaning what?"

"I mean if you thought putting recipes online was unfulfilling, you should try law school. Jesus H."

"Why'd you go?"

"What else am I gonna do? Have you heard the one about my sister the masseuse–folk singer–duck boat operator? I mean, the Andersons are comfortable, but I don't think they can support both of us *and* keep themselves in the style they're accustomed to. Look, if I don't get this job, I'm cashing it all in and getting a fishing boat down in Mexico. You laugh," he said. Actually, she had frowned. "But I'm serious. Fuck it."

"Why not just do that now?"

"I mean, I'm not totally over everything quite yet, you know, air conditioning and designer suits. Also, I spent a summer in Veracruz when I was in college, and you could not find butter anywhere. But if I head down that way, I'll send you a postcard. You can visit my shack. You're not allergic to seafood, are you?"

Lying in bed that night, feeling wired, Liselle imagined the shack on the coast. She remembered a daydream she'd had back during the time of Selena. It was of them in a New York brownstone with large windows and a fluffy black dog. Though she was awake, the sound of the ringing phone on her nightstand alarmed her. Her first thought was that it was Verity with terrible news. Or maybe it would be her repentant father.

"You awake?" said a male voice. White. "Please excuse me. I'm a touch inebriated. Intoxicated. There are so many lovely words for this feeling—"

"*Winn?*"

She felt strange talking to him in the dark. She pulled the covers up around her. "Do we know each other well enough to call drunk in the middle of the night?"

"'Drunk,' on the other hand, is not a lovely word. Your city has many fine drinking establishments, by the way. Anyway, this call has a purpose. A query."

Merely curious, Liselle knew it was her job to sound annoyed. "What?"

"If I get this job, should I really move to Philadelphia? It seems kind of . . . lonely here. Like, no offense, you seem lonely." Suddenly he sounded sober.

"Why don't you just get your boat in Mexico? I'm sure the local fishing community will welcome you."

"Really I'm just asking you this: If I come to Philadelphia, will you be my friend? I think you'd make, like, a really good friend."

Liselle yawned, though she felt wide awake.

"I'll be your friend."

◎ ◎ **21** ◎ ◎

You sure are spending a lot of time with this gay white man," said Verity a few months later.

After Winn moved to Philadelphia, he and Liselle became constants. They talked on the phone like middle school girls and went downtown to watch art house movies: *Rushmore*, *The Thin Red Line*, and a revival of *Thelma & Louise*. Liselle showed Winn South Street, where he complained about the grease smell and the grimy kids begging with their dogs. "Why would anyone come here on purpose?" he asked, unimpressed by the folk art gallery or the hat store. On more successful outings, she took him to Robin's Books or to Rittenhouse Square Park; they saw the Roots and Digable Planets perform at Electric Factory; once, when they were downtown, she pointed out the Gallery mall, afraid that if she stepped inside she would revert to an awkward teenager attending Masterman and living with her mother.

"I'm showing him the city," Liselle told Verity. "What does gay have to do with anything? Besides, I don't think he's gay."

"But you are, right? Gay?"

Liselle queried herself, as she often did, about why she spoke to Verity as much as she did. But she did not ask herself why she was spending so much time with Winn. She knew why: it was fun. He made a mockery of most aspects of his life: his staid family, the arrogant idiots at the firm where he worked. When she told him about the dreariness of her childhood, the routine deprivations of being Black, female, and gay in America, his interest made it all an ironic, hilarious story. Instead of swelling, tragic strings in the background, there was only his laughter. And he always paid for dinner.

There was another thread between them. Once, during a twenty-five-dollar cab ride back to her house from downtown, Winn had said, "I don't know why, but you make me feel calm." This moved Liselle, who'd been nicknamed for a predator, who'd tried to throw a woman out of a window, who'd wound up alone.

One weekend Winn couldn't hang out because he had a date with someone named Shannon.

"I can't tell if that name is pretentious or trashy for a white person," Liselle said to Winn the next Friday at a happy hour in a little Manayunk bar by the river. Many of the doors they darkened she would never have ventured through as a Black woman alone.

He laughed. "What did Shannon ever do to you? She's just an innocent, breasty paralegal from New Jersey."

Liselle thought about how she'd tried to get a job as a paralegal, the extreme femme-ness of the women at that office, the secretaries, paralegals, *and* the sole woman lawyer. She shook her head. "I thought you were better than that."

"Am I, though?" Winn said. "She's the same age as me. It's not *Working Girl* or any of those Melanie Griffith movies. Did you see the one where the father hires her as a prostitute for his—"

"But do you think that's good for your profile at the firm?"

"Honestly, I think fucking a paralegal might be a requirement for making partner there. And it's safer than dating one of the married lawyers."

"Maybe you shouldn't think of your job as a dating service. I think people are even using the internet for that now."

"As usual, you are the soul of reason, Liselle. And yet there's just something about Shannon."

It was a languid Friday evening near the end of summer. The sun burned florid outside the barred windows. The air hung thick with cigarette smoke and air conditioning. A man wove over to the jukebox, selected the song "Wicked Game," and began dancing with himself. Guitar sounds flooded the room with mournfulness. "Go home, Larry," the bartender said, sounding weary. "You're making it unhappy hour."

Liselle knew Winn would put down stakes at his soulless job, turn in his long-term rental car, and move into a sleek place being renovated downtown. He would no longer live in the motel-like corporate apartments by the airport and be so willing to head up Lincoln Drive to retrieve her for adventures in fine living. School and teaching would start again. She would laugh less. Then he would get caught up in various melodramas with various paralegals; she would have no one to talk to.

"I have to get a fucking life," she said. The bartender moved away from them.

They watched Larry's jagged dancing. He howled along with Chris Isaak. *Nobody loves no one.* It reminded Liselle of a loud song Winn liked to play where the singer kept shouting, *There is! No! Love! In! This! World! Anymore* . . .

"Hey," Winn said suddenly. "I have an idea. You know I'm moving next week, but I'm going to slit my wrists if I have to spend another weekend at that fluorescent-lit dungeon where I'm staying. What if I spring for a weekend at the Ritz-Carlton and you come crash with me?"

Liselle felt a sensation so mixed she wouldn't name it. "Oh, whatever. Why don't you invite *Shannon*?"

He looked at her as if from the sides of his eyes. "Yes, ours is a beautiful love story, Shannon and mine, but to be honest we've only been on two dates. Anyway, I want *you* to come."

She looked at him. "You know I'm a lesbian, right?" she said, thinking in quick succession of a number of women she'd been with, holding their hands, looking into their eyes, the grip of their thighs; her last thought was of Selena.

Winn snorted. "Oh, Liselle, I'm not trying to fuck you. I'm trying to have a fancy sleepover. We can do each other's hair and shit."

"I will never let you touch my hair," said Liselle.

And she never did, not when they decided to "try doing sex" (his words) forty minutes before checkout time at the Ritz-Carlton, or even years later when she had just given birth to Patrice after three hours' hard labor, and Winn was reaching over to give her a strange head pat. She managed to block him with her elbow, without jostling the tiny alien in her arms.

"What?" he cried. "You did a good job!"

⦿◎ 22 ◎⦿

Soon after their hotel weekend, Liselle found herself headed to a cabin in Maine, a new and bizarre style of vacation for her. On the way, however, they were stopping for lunch at Winn's family home in the West End of Hartford.

The house was full of dark wood furniture from various historical eras. They initially sat on hard chairs, drinking sour lemonade in the humid un-air-conditioned den and eventually moved to the darker but not cooler dining room. Aware that Winn's family was wealthy, Liselle tried not to look perplexed by the menu of tuna fish sandwiches and cold, grainy tomato soup.

"My parents honeymooned in Spain. So it's not summer around here until we have gazpacho," Winn said.

"You are correct," said Winn's dad. "And the best gazpacho is my Lynnie's gazpacho."

"Well, actually, the tomatoes aren't quite good yet," the mother said, blushing. "I got this from that new gourmet grocery in West Hartford. You know where I got those lime bars that time? They have really good prepared foods."

Winn's dad made a sound in his throat. "This is *almost* as good as yours. Not quite, but almost."

Winn's mom stood. "Could use some salt, right? Anybody want salt?"

"Sit down and enjoy your lunch, Lynnie," said Winn's dad. "You've been fussing around all morning." (*Making tuna fish?* thought Liselle.) "We'll get by without the salt. You know *I* can't have any."

"Dr. Lang says Dad has to watch his salt," she said to Winn, taking her seat again.

"You don't seem like you need any salt, either, Winn," said his dad. "Have you had your numbers checked lately?"

"Dad, I'm not even thirty," he said, flushing slightly. "I don't 'check my numbers.'"

"Liselle," said Winn's dad, "don't let my boy kill himself with his devil-may-care attitude."

"That's a little dramatic, George," Winn's mom said mildly. "But, Winn, when *was* the last time you had a physical? It's not that . . . it's just important to take care of yourself."

Winn drummed his fingers on the table. "Let's move on to more interesting topics. For instance, you might ask Liselle about herself."

Liselle's cheeks burned under George's and Lynnie's gazes. "I'm sorry," said Winn's father, though he looked distinctly unapologetic. "It's just that we see so little of our son."

"You see even less of Jennifer or Jandy or whatever she's calling herself now," Winn retorted rather fiercely. Liselle didn't know much about his older sister except the crucial detail that she drove him crazy. He kept trying to tell stories that Liselle knew were supposed to enrage her, but she couldn't figure out the central issue between them.

"Liselle," the mother said, ignoring Winn's outburst, "how is your sandwich? There's not too much celery, is there?"

"Everything is great," she lied, though there was a lot of celery, which she despised.

"So, Bryn Mawr," said George Anderson. "A lot of . . . girls there. Did you like that?"

Liselle felt an irrational terror in her throat. Had Winn told his father about her life before him?

"Ew, Dad," said Winn, growing decidedly younger with each moment in his parents' home.

"George is a terrible sexist," said Lynnie, smiling. "He's a lot better than when we met, though, aren't you, George?"

"Sexism is a dying art," said George. "Like chivalry. In fact, it is chivalry."

"Jesus," Winn muttered. "No wonder friggin' Jandy never comes around."

"Your sister loves doors being held for her. And I don't think it's 'Jandy' anymore. I think it's back to 'Jennifer.' But we'll find out for sure next month."

"George," said Winn's mother, beginning to color faintly.

"What?" Winn barked. "Are you all preparing for one of her much-anticipated, highly publicized no-shows? Have you contacted the *West Hartford Tattler*?"

"Now, Winn," said Winn's mom.

Winn turned to Liselle. "Once a year my sister says she's going to come home, and then a lot of complicated plans are made, farm animals are slaughtered for burned offerings, and then she gets some mysterious illness or a sudden new job even though she is the most perpetually unemployed adult and—"

"We're actually going to visit *her* this time," said Winn's dad, with a hint of pride.

Winn's mother made another noise. His father continued. "She's going to host us in this little French village where she's been staying. She's met someone and apparently it's serious. A widower, high up in the telecom industry." He cleared his throat.

"Is that right?" said Winn, looking back and forth between his parents. "A family vacation with three-fourths of the family, huh?"

His father looked amused. "We haven't traveled together, the four of us, what? Since you were in college."

"We didn't have the chance to tell you," said his mom, twisting a napkin. "We didn't invite you only because, well, you're starting this new job and everything . . ." She trailed off, looking at Liselle. "My goodness, we really have been terrible hosts. Maybe you all can stay the night. We really do want to get to know you, Lisette."

"It's Liselle," snapped Winn.

"It's okay," said Liselle.

"Oh dear, I'm sorry," Winn's mother said.

"I once knew a girl named *Liesl*," said Winn's father in a once-upon-a-time voice. "Liesl Schneider. Her family had come from Austria after the war. My parents were very suspicious of her parents, if you know what I mean."

"Oh, wait, is this the part of the lunch where we talk about the Nazis we've known?" Winn laughed. "Let's go back a moment to the subject of Jennifer. Is the relationship serious or is this 'widower'"— he used air quotes—"seriously wealthy and you think it's a good idea for her to support herself by sponging off an old man?"

Winn's dad's eyes sparkled with mischief. "I know someone else who sponged off an old man for many years."

"Thanks for lunch," said Winn. He pushed away his bowl, which looked full.

His father said, "Calm down, boy. You know I'm joking."

Liselle could see gears shifting in Winn's head. She could feel him trying to decide whether to blow up the afternoon. Not wanting to be in those smoking ruins, she attempted to radiate the calmness he supposedly found in her. He leaned back in his chair.

Winn's dad spoke again, this time to Liselle. "So, did Winn tell you I grew up on the Main Line? Not so far from your alma

mater. Out there would have been a good place to hide as an escaped Nazi."

"I wonder about that sometimes myself," said Winn. "Honey, we
should probably get on the road soon if we're going to make it to the
cabin tonight."

"Okay," she said. *Honey?*

Winn's mother shook her head vigorously. "Stay just a bit longer. Aunt Gladys was planning to stop by and show us pictures from
her Lake District trip. How long has it been since you've seen her,
Winnie?"

Winn laughed. "Gladys? Mom, that is *not* a way to get me to
stay."

"Well, I have dessert," she said with a panicked look. "Let me
serve you some dessert. Does anybody want coffee?"

"Darling, you know better than anybody what coffee in the
afternoon does to my stomach," said Winn's dad.

"Coffee sounds good, Mom," said Winn. "I can make it."

Then Liselle was sitting at the dining room table with George
Anderson and he was asking her what she'd studied, how she liked
teaching middle school students, what her parents did. He said he'd
once considered teaching, but lacked the patience. He did not pry
when she made it clear that her father was no one to her. They chatted politely, but she felt like a shape-shifting creature under her
pasted smile: a picture she'd once seen of Sarah Baartman/the emotionally intelligent Black prostitute in *St. Elmo's Fire*/a monkey/
a uniformed scholarship student in *Sarafina!*/Verity . . .

Winn and his mother came back with sweet strawberries and
dry, pale cake. Liselle passed on the coffee, for much the same reason as her future father-in-law. She wondered if there could be any
other possible commonalities between her and this particular individual of that distant species, the wealthy old white man.

As they pulled out of the driveway, Liselle looked back to see

Mr. Anderson squinting with his arms folded, and Lynnie waving energetically.

"Did you enjoy your lunch with the Andersons?" asked Winn.

"Did that happen?" Liselle asked. She meant to say it to herself, but Winn was there.

"Now you're family."

"Please don't call me honey anymore. It made me feel like . . ."

"Made you feel like you were in a diorama with the Andersons? In the *Caucasians of Connecticut* natural history exhibit? I enjoyed your enthusiastic smiling. You fit right in," Winn said, an edge to his voice.

"Are we having our first fight?" asked Liselle. "What is it about?"

"I guess I'm fighting with myself. I just can't believe how much I let them get to me about Jennifer."

"Jandy?"

Winn laughed. "No, seriously, before this she was down in Austin trying to become a singer with that name. I didn't make that up."

"That's the best part of your family so far. The name 'Jandy.'"

"I know. I should kill her," Winn said lightly. "Just kidding."

"Did you have to say 'just kidding'?"

They laughed.

23

Almost fifteen years before what would likely be their final dinner party, maybe in another life, Liselle and Winn sat on a small emerald green velvet love seat in an alcove, off to the side of the large reception hall at the downtown hotel where they would celebrate being married. A wedding band played upbeat jazz. The DJ that Liselle had wanted would come later. Winn's dad, who was of course paying for the wedding, had taken an unusual interest in the planning. He thought DJs were classless. "I mean, if you're not going to have a live band, why not just pay some *dude* to bring in one of those *ghetto* blasters?" ("Dad," Winn said, a toothless warning.) But the only thing Liselle had really wanted was a DJ that she could pester with her lengthy playlist ideas, and Winn's mom intervened on her behalf. Later she found out (they all did) that Mrs. Anderson had known she was dying of stomach cancer at the time of the planning. After she was gone, it moved Liselle to think of her fighting for the DJ when she had so little time left on earth. It was not less moving when she discovered that while Winn's dad was a very successful insurance man, Winn's mother was the one whose family money sustained their entire life, including a trust fund that paid for things like weekends at the Ritz-Carlton.

The ceremony, at a local Episcopal church, had gone well. Though there had been some uncomfortable spaces between his words, the minister, as old and white as a ghost, hadn't said anything too off-putting. Verity, who was aggressively friendly with Winn and his family, hadn't frowned, and the unity candle hadn't set the altar afire. In the aftermath, "wife" sighed with relief and leaned against "husband"—but found that his body felt rigid and unwelcoming. She pulled away to look at him. "What's up?"

"Liselle," said Winn, in a thick voice. "Did we just do something terrible? I mean—did you really want to do this?"

Liselle hugged her bare arms, suddenly cold. She felt the complicated underthings from the wedding store cutting into her torso. "What are you asking me? Did *you?*"

"Well, I'm the one who proposed. In fact, I proposed everything from the beginning. I'm asking what *you* wanted."

"Winn," she said, panicking, a shadow in the corners of her eyes threatening to blot out her vision. "I *did* what I wanted. What the hell?"

She could see the photographer approaching, Winn's mother at his side, looking worried, as always. They were going to take photos with Winn's rich, racist grandma, who unfailingly called her Lisa and became irritable when corrected. (The other grandma, racist and not rich, had stayed in Fresno.)

"Well, we can take these expensive pictures as a souvenir," said Liselle, feeling the spirit of Verity in her, "and then we can hammer out a divorce."

"You know that's not what I meant," Winn said. "I'm never divorcing you," he said dramatically.

"Isn't it a little early to be renewing our vows?"

"That's funny. Yeah, that's a good one," Winn said solemnly.

The image of Liselle's father, sitting across from her at the bakery, came into her head. In a rough motion she took Winn's arm to make a formal entrance into the hall. She knew he was not seriously reconsidering their marriage, but the conversation gave her the beginnings of a headache.

Thinking of the evening as their last date, Liselle was at turns mechanical and reckless. A smile that did not reach her eyes for photos, gratitude and platitudes offered at all the tables they visited. A stiff first dance to "Heroes" by David Bowie, which Winn thought would be cool. Of course, it sounded insane and desperate because the song was meant to sound insane and desperate, no matter how the young wedding singer tried to sweeten it. Nihilism flooding her body, Liselle drank champagne and played with Winn's cousin Daisy's beautiful hair. Then the DJ finally took over, put on Marvin Gaye, and she invited Mr. Charles to dance. Verity glared from the sidelines; Liselle knew full well that "Come Get to This" was one of her mother's favorites.

Mr. Charles was effusive. "I think this might be the best wedding I've ever been to, besides my buddy's where Robert Bell played."

"Thank you, Mr. Charles." Liselle had heard him speak of that wedding many times, and despite her general distaste for him, she could not help feeling honored that hers was in a league with it.

"You know Robert Bell from Kool & the Gang?"

Nearby, Winn's mother danced with Gladys. Though they were old, thin, and delicate, the two women seemed roguish together, holding hands.

"You look just like a princess," Mr. Charles was saying. "I told your mother you'd find your way. I been tellin' her. And don't let anybody say anything to you about the interracial fact, because if you catch ahold of something good, you can't let go. These men out here ain't shit," he said, reminding Liselle of something Verity often said of Mr. Charles.

"Excuse me, Mr. Charles," Liselle said, and headed into the mercifully empty bathroom. She tried to negotiate the full skirt of her ridiculous lace gown—she'd essentially let Verity pick it out—to get herself onto a toilet in a cramped stall. She wondered how many women brewed up wedding-day yeast infections in sweat-soaked underwear, as she struggled to peel off the fifty-dollar slip of cotton. She threw it in the little box meant for menstrual trash and left the stall.

In the bathroom mirror, she saw her dreadlocked updo in the first stages of collapse. It was obvious that her and Winn being together was crazy. But he had kept upping the ante, moving quickly to get out ahead of second thoughts and boredom, and she had kept accepting the challenge. Their alliance was a conspiracy against the various imprisoning realities they'd known. She began taking out hairpins and throwing them onto the floor. The last time she'd littered, she had been six and Verity had grabbed her by the neck.

Selena materialized next to her in the mirror and stood looking mutely at Liselle. She did that sometimes. But it was only four months, so long ago. *Why are you still here?* Liselle jumped when the bathroom door whipped open.

"I see there's a whole other party going on in here," said Jennifer. She had given a toast earlier, claiming that Winn was the glue bonding the Anderson family, and that Liselle was the glue that held Winn together. The speech had almost made her cry—especially since she knew she had to leave him.

"Yeah," Liselle said, feeling nervous. "There's a lot going on here." She gestured toward her hair and dress. "I mean, this is not really my usual situation."

Jennifer laughed and addressed Liselle in the mirror. "I don't think this is anyone's usual situation. I've never understood bride drag. White means death in so many cultures. But," she said, with a little smile, "you look amazing. You should always wear white at your weddings."

Jennifer wasn't quite pretty with her sharp ferret's face and her large eyebrows. And yet her silky blue slip dress made everyone else look like a fat frump or a sad cake. And there was something . . . one could even see how she could pull off the name "Jandy." Liselle wanted to sleep with her. And Liselle knew that Jennifer *wanted* her to want to sleep with her, which was irritating. Not then, nor ever, did she figure out how Winn's parents, with their unpolished, uptight white northeasterner routine, had given birth to such little operators.

"Later, Jennifer," Liselle said, escaping the bathroom.

"Liselle," Jennifer murmured.

After ten o'clock, as the party neared its end, Liselle approached the DJ and made a request that had not been on the lengthy email she'd sent him (*cool, hot, cool,* she'd written, characterizing each song in case he wanted to make substitutions). Then she pulled Winn out of the seat where he was huddled with some one-syllable guys from the firm, Biff and Gim, or whatever.

"Our last dance," she said as the opening moans of "Forever My Lady" filled the room. "Our last dance ever." She had not meant to say this. She had been writing a letter in her head that she planned to leave in the honeymoon suite before slipping away.

"You know I didn't mean what I said, babe. I was just nervous."

She spoke sternly. "Winn, it's traditional to be nervous *before* the wedding, but not okay to ruin the reception."

"Sorry, sorry. I know I spazzed back there. Look," he said, taking her by the hands and looking into her eyes. "I'll make it up to you with the life we're going to have. I'm so fucking happy right now." He smelled like pure alcohol. She herself was largely composed of champagne at this point. Together, they were flammable.

Later, instead of having sex, they would take turns vomiting into their glistening honeymoon suite toilet. Liselle did not write the letter. She told herself she had forever to do that.

"You look amazing, by the way," he breathed, pulling her closer on the dance floor. She listened to the extended synthesizer solo at the end of "Forever My Lady" and thought again about Selena, with pity and also longing.

24

t times, Liselle remembered being waited on by tuxedoed white servers at Le Bec-Fin at her first wedding anniversary, the heavy, gleaming silver dessert cart. She thought about how the ability to select and eat a confection from that cart made her part of something not larger, but smaller.

She didn't like to think it, but it was hard to imagine herself there with another woman, especially a Black woman.

She didn't like to think it, but while there were Black men in the city who might occasionally go to Le Bec-Fin, she was sure none would have taken *her* there.

In college, she'd read *Soul on Ice*, which she'd known was the self-serving, homophobic raving of a rapist, but the formulations nagged at her. Liselle wasn't willowy or light-skinned. She'd insisted on natural hair, having cut off her perm after sleeping with her first woman. Old pictures of her with straightened hair looked ridiculous and somehow sad. They also made her look like the frequently bewigged Verity.

Pressed up against a woman, her face buried in a woman, she had definitely felt like a woman. Certain Black men made her feel, in their treatment of her, like a weak man. They gave other women seats on the el as Liselle stood balancing heavy bags. They looked at the girls she was with and then at her, their lips curled with disdain, but without violent intent. If Liselle was visible to them, she was neither appealing nor challenging.

Liselle remembered the weekend she and Winn had spent together in the Ritz-Carlton, their first real date. French fries in fluffy bathrobes, action movies, the glaring Black bellhop who wheeled the room service cart recklessly, (lightly) bruising Winn's shin. Liselle had wanted to tell him they weren't even having sex, because mostly they weren't. Not yet.

Winn was the first (and last) man Liselle slept with. He'd seemed disappointed that her hymen was already broken and that there would be no blood.

"What are you, a Viking?" she'd asked him as they lay there in the white sheets.

"You are my Valhalla," he said. It was a joke, but it flattered her.

25

When Patrice was born, things Verity had said to Liselle suddenly made sense. Liselle had always thought these old anecdotes had been Verity's admission that she was dead inside and that she had never properly loved Liselle. Things like "Once I left you in the crib screaming by yourself at night and walked to the corner," or "I thought about hurting you, that first year, but I didn't."

Liselle finally understood things she had been told but not felt. That when she had been born, her father was out many nights, working events at the Spectrum and at Veterans Stadium, and that he often slept during the day. When Patrice was born, Winn had just started at a new firm, one where he made considerably more money, but where there was more vicious competition for partner. He took three days off for the birth, asked a lot of questions in order to change maybe three diapers, and then disappeared.

One day when Liselle was healed enough to move around, she packed a diaper bag and actually got herself out of the house. She loaded Patrice into the car and drove him to Chestnut Hill. There, on Germantown Avenue, she thought of her messy house as a dark cavern; she was haunted by a blues-tinged animated children's special she'd once seen about John Henry. As she pushed the stroller slowly around other pedestrians and into the April wind, it hit her. *Everybody on this street has had a mother.* She blinked and it was still true. The rotund bald Black man walking by, a mustached white man at his side; the wizened white woman with a cane and incongruous glossy blonde hair; the deliveryman in shorts with bright red frost-bitten legs. All of them. She couldn't believe the things everybody's mother had done: their bleeding bodies, sleep-deprived minds, their spit-up-speckled loose-fitting clothes, their unkempt hair, their reduction to shrill nags. If a child lived to see adulthood, then even many of the bad mothers, the ones strung out on crack, had still done a hell of a lot for a child. The children who'd been adopted had been tended by combinations of women. And those women did—*we* did, *we* do, thought Liselle—all this for someone, really something, that did not care for them. Something that cared only if they died—until someone else came along with warm milk.

Of course, no one asked to be born, either. This was a thought she'd cultivated at a young age as a defense against Verity's guilt trips.

She and Patrice walked up the block, popping into boutiques where she could manage the stroller, finally deciding to go into the bakery—the same one where she'd met up with her father a few years ago, in another lifetime. The father who'd left Verity alone so many nights with a baby and then for good with a toddler. Patrice looked calm if not happy, his black button eyes taking it in, his alien hands moving occasionally in contemplation. Liselle sat at a small table, gently moving the stroller back and forth to keep him interested and make him forget about nursing. She thought of the baby as a time bomb because she was still trying to understand how she would manage a life where she was expected to pull out her breast every two to four hours. She thought about Verity, who had waved away the idea of breastfeeding. "I just couldn't sit still for that," she'd said.

A few minutes later, Liselle felt a sense of triumph, reflecting that she'd eaten a large (cardboard-tasting) cookie and Patrice hadn't

freaked out. As she moved past their table on her way out, two elderly women in hats cooed. "What a good baby," one of them said,
extending her sandpaper-brown hand in approval. Liselle thanked
them, nearly tearing up. It gobsmacked her. Old Black women, the
mothers of us all, had mothers. Even Verity's mother, who'd died
when Liselle was a baby. Even Verity.

It was time to head back to the cave for his and her naps, but first
Liselle navigated her way into a kitchen supply store that was really
too small for the stroller. A white woman at the cash register with
a particularly thin smile greeted her loudly and asked if she was
looking for anything in particular. Patrice began twisting himself
in a warning fashion.

Then the woman exclaimed, "Ooh, he's a fresh one. How long
have you been taking care of him?"

She looked at the woman in confusion. "Taking care of . . ." Angry little noises began to come from the stroller, veering toward a
full-blown protest. Liselle got out of the store. "That bitch," she said
to Patrice, whose newborn hair was sandy-colored. He punched the
air with his fists, emitting a thin wail.

Later that night, after she was able to get Patrice down for a few
hours, instead of taking her precious night nap (a sad parody of a
"disco nap"), she called her mother, who might or might not have
been asleep.

"I get it, Ma. I get it now. I'm sorry about being a baby."

"What now?"

"Look, I don't mean acting immature; I mean I'm sorry for
being a baby that you had to take care of."

"Hold on there!" Verity yelled. "Don't touch my baby. I'm coming over."

"You don't need to come over."

"Is that Winn there? Y'all okay? I'm coming over!"

"I think at this point you should stop calling him 'that Winn,'"

Liselle said, though it was an upgrade from "that gay white man." "And you don't need to come over. I'm just apologizing."

"Now, start from the beginning. What is it you called for?"

"That I'm sorry for everything I did to you as a baby. That I finally understand all of what you warned me about."

"You sound crazy. Where *is* Winn, anyway?"

Liselle had to say, as she often did, that he was working and that it was just her. And Patrice.

26

In the dining room, Liselle found herself wondering if the FBI used handcuffs and what she would say to Patrice as his father was led away. Then she tuned herself back into the conversation. Vanessa was describing a cruise to Croatia and Liza kept asking why anyone would ever want to visit a country with so many recent mass graves. Gary smiled at Liza being Liza. Ron and Gladys came back to the table from their tête-à-tête about Gladys's money, which Liselle thought was her cue to free Xochitl; she excused herself to go find her wallet.

Cash in hand from her bedroom, she then passed Patrice's room and heard a noise. She stood still to listen and then heard it again. She yanked the door open and yelped, startled by a bear sitting in the dark on the bed, holding a tumbler.

"You were right," Winn said. "This party is depressing."

Turning on the overhead light, she saw there was a lollipop dipped into his glass; the effect was a parody of an olive in a martini. She spoke sternly. "You scared the shit out of me. Also, you just left everybody downstairs."

"Or did they leave me up here?"

"I guess you're drunk."

"You know I hate that word. But not really," he said, pulling out the candy and popping it into his mouth. "That might be the problem. Maybe I should get trashed and go down there naked, take a shit on the living room floor. 'Cause if I did that, then nobody would even try to talk me into going through this again."

Liselle swallowed hard. "Is somebody trying to get you to run for office again?"

"Not yet. But they will. They invested so much in me. Though Gladys thought it was a loan." He laughed. "I bet she thinks if I win next time, she'll get interest."

Liselle felt taken aback by the layers of his cluelessness. First of all, his loss had been definitive. It was clear his future lay in continuing to oversee boring, unethical, but "basically legal" land agreements for rich people, and then maybe consulting. He lacked the charisma and magnetism to propel himself beyond the small rooms where people enjoyed drinking cocktails he mixed. Politics did not need him.

Second, he had not the slightest idea about the wheels in motion and the possibility of being ground under them. Yes, this was Liselle's fault, but she still found his total lack of awareness profoundly disorienting.

As she struggled to keep from leaving her body, he continued to share his reflections. "I don't know. I mean, the president is one thing. I mean, if a guy like that was going to get on the *Harvard Law Review*, he was going to be president. That guy's a fucking unicorn. But somebody like me? Somebody like us?"

"Us," Liselle said.

"I'm not saying I lost because of you and Patrice or anything, obviously."

"Yeah, I'm not sure how that would work."

"Well, I'm just saying—I guess—remember that thing Mr. Charles said to you that one time, about 'the interracial fact' . . ." At this he took the half-eaten lollipop out of his mouth and tossed it with accuracy into Patrice's wastepaper basket.

"Layup," he muttered.

"Winn." Liselle sighed, moving Patrice's pillow out of the way to sit down on the edge of the bed. "The FBI is indicting you for corruption."

The color drained from Winn's face. "What?"

"You're being indicted for corruption. But I don't know why. Can you tell me why?"

"Is this a joke?"

She chose her words carefully. "A man named William Mc-Michael got in touch with me about this."

"He called you?"

She sat down next to him. "Well, yes, he called me, but I had— I had met him before."

Winn shook himself. But he still had a look of astonishment and horror. "Tell me everything. Start at the beginning."

She told him about the restaurant fundraiser. They'd made small talk; he was Black.

"How is that relevant?" asked Winn.

"I guess it's not."

Thinking of Scheherazade, she dragged out her story because the coffee shop meeting, where William McMichael had asked questions, had been over two months ago. Sixty-plus days when she could have told Winn that federal law enforcement was looking into his associates and doings.

"When did you have coffee together?" His voice was nasty.

"Winn, we didn't—"

"When was it?"

No sooner had she muttered "February" than he grabbed both her biceps and began squeezing them. He got very close to her face. *"What the fuck is wrong with you?"*

"Let me go," she said, trying to keep her voice steady. She imagined bringing the party guests to them with her screams.

He took his hands off her and put his face in them. "What did you tell them?" he said, his voice muffled.

"About what? I don't know anything. What is there to know, Winn? That's what I was wondering."

"Oh, ho. That's why you didn't say anything to me. Because you were pissed that I kept some insignificant shit from you. And you believed that whatever this guy was saying was true. Is that about right?"

She hadn't allowed these feelings to crystallize as thoughts. But he had named them reasonably well. They stared at each other, both breathing heavily.

"You know, Liselle, I know you have a little lump of ice for a fucking heart, which, to be honest, I always kind of liked about you. And I get that you don't give a shit about me, but don't you think this might affect Patrice? Don't you think the fallout here might be a problem for our son?"

"Patrice will be fine," said Liselle. "Winn, we still have people downstairs, but can you tell me—just—what did you do?"

"*I didn't do anything!*" he screamed. Though she had fumed that the installation people had overcharged them, Liselle was grateful for the sound system that was piping Terence Blanchard through the house, the trumpet wailing for a drowned New Orleans.

"Look," Winn said. "I took a couple of meetings with Jack Leggett, the developer, and, I mean, he asked for the kinds of assurances developers ask politicians for . . ." Winn shook his head with increasing violence, turning almost a mulberry color.

Being with Winn had allowed Liselle to glide into places she never would have dreamed of going. A luxury ski lodge in Idaho? But she had always hated that she had married someone whose face could change in that particular way. How had people with such an obvious tell taken over the world?

"So, if you didn't do anything, why are these people looking for you?"

"Given what you've done, your *treachery*, I don't know that you deserve an explanation. But you might feel vindicated to know that this falls into the category of 'the bitch set me up.'"

"You can't call me that."

He rolled his eyes. "You're not the bitch. This is some bitch who tried to sleep with me. Leggett's daughter."

"What?" said Liselle. "Who?"

Winn said nothing, letting her spin her wheels. This would have been a new one from the campaign, maybe wearing one of the small run of Win-Winn T-shirts. There had been a volunteer Ron brought around who wore a distracting amount of perfume; the roots of her blond hair had been dark; her Win-Winn T-shirt was at least a size too small. She had been just out of college, but dressed like a middle-aged woman in a Talbots catalog. She was forever smiling with lipstick on her teeth, giving the appearance of someone casting about after a career in local TV news didn't work out. Winn had seemed animated around her, but Liselle had always thought he was trying to mask his sexist condescension, because she was corny as shit. Now Liselle remembered that Winn had said they shouldn't invite her tonight, and Liselle had thought that was odd because she never would have invited her. She tried to think of the girl's name; it was strange, illiterate-sounding.

"Was it, was her name—Amberly? That white girl? Her last name—"

"She's Leggett's daughter from his first marriage. Anyway, we didn't even sleep together. I stopped it. And would you be happier if she was Black? What do you even care? You weren't thinking about me when you were canoodling with the feds in the coffee shop."

After several years of relative numbness, Liselle had experienced a number of rare emotions during the time of the campaign, new kinds of performance anxiety, shame, anticipation, a bit of wild hope. Liselle knew Jack Leggett's name from buildings throughout the city—also from occasional newspaper stories about low-rent scandals involving charter schools and the city council. Now their fates were connected because her husband "didn't even sleep" with his daughter. In the first few seconds of absorbing this reality, Liselle anticipated a cyclone of loathing (for him and for herself; for them) just about to touch her, but was still calm enough to say, "*Ew.*"

"What do you care?" he hissed.

"What do you mean, what do I care?"

"What. Do. You. Care? Can you even remember the last time we fucked?"

Liselle spoke softly. "Winn. I still don't understand what's happening. And, incidentally, I do remember. Do you?"

It had been a month ago, after an unusually crowded and energetic campaign event at Quaker Academy. Liselle had been worried that holding an event there would send the wrong message—the school had a fifty-thousand-dollar tuition. But the principal, her boss, had looked awed when she swept in at Winn's side. Chris had delivered some of his congregants to help pack the event. The a capella choir had performed "Happy" to a crowded gym and there was spontaneous double-time clapping. For the first time Liselle heard the song's melancholy undercurrents, which actually made her happy.

Later that night, tipsy with success and some almost-flat prosecco, they'd had raucous sex, the likes of which hadn't happened in years. Liselle had a hazy memory of slapping Winn in the face while she was on top of him. She realized now, with some combination of nausea and rage, that he'd probably been involved with this girl and that was what had excited him. Her first ménage à trois and nobody had bothered to tell her.

"Look, like I told you, I met with Leggett through Ron."

"Ron," said Liselle.

Winn rolled his eyes. "Ron had me meet with Leggett because that's what people in my situation do—they meet with Leggett and tell him what he wants to hear. And his daughter started working for the campaign, wagging her little ass in my face."

Her little flat *ass*, Liselle recalled, shaking her head slowly. She had never thought this would be Winn. Yes, he was a WASP (WASP-ish: his paternal great-grandmother had had a Catholic father, who'd left the family and disappeared into history) in middle life. But Liselle had thought the politics was enough of a sports car, enough of a midlife cliché, if there was going to be one. But she had never found Winn cliché. After all, he'd chosen her—a Black woman of substance, a lesbian. Liselle!

And yet.

"You are truly an asshole," she said, wondering how they were going to go downstairs together.

He shrugged. "Well, you were supposed to fix that, remember? You were supposed to keep me from turning into Jandy." Jennifer had sent them a campaign donation of forty-five dollars and the check had bounced. "Anyway, I guess we all have our secrets, huh?"

She stood and began backing away from him. "I'm going to, just, I'm going to go." She stepped out of Patrice's room (poor Patrice!), nervous about turning her back on Winn. Looking at him, she saw herself all those years ago, packing up her little overnight things at the Ritz-Carlton. While Winn took a long shower, singing "Under Pressure," both Freddie Mercury's and David Bowie's parts, an ATM slip had fallen from his pants. Liselle had picked it up and the number had lodged in her brain, all those zeros in a lousy checking account. Liselle told herself that this information had not changed anything she'd done (*it had not, it had not, it had not*). She was thinking about all those zeros—still—as she moved slowly away from him.

He'd said to her, a couple of weeks after the hotel, "I really think we could be something together. Something really original."

For all that deliberate stepping, her heel caught in a worn part of the floor and she fell down the stairs.

elena dismounted the number 65 bus and paused to get organized. Clutching a bag of sticky buns for her parents in one hand, she used the other to nick another string off the cuff of her hooded sweatshirt, a green thing going gray that she'd had for almost twenty years. Mrs. DaSilva at the bakery had kept offering to replace it until finally Selena stopped wearing it to work. She adopted the habit of putting it on in the morning, taking it off before she got to work, and putting it back on before she left for home. Her other boss, Scott, who supervised her on an office cleaning crew in the evenings, never bothered her about it. No one there cared much what she wore, though the women eyed her uneasily if she forgot to take her hood off when she entered the building.

"Mom," she called out, closing the door behind her. As usual, the faint sound of a commercial targeting the old, sick, and under-employed was the answer. After a long career with the Philadelphia public schools as a teacher and then a counselor, Alethia Octave had retired six years ago, bubbling about book clubs, cruises, the gym. Selena knew that her mother blamed her for the fact that she'd done mostly nothing since then except get up a little later and watch day-time television, a practice she had once considered a category of sin.

Meanwhile her father had been on track to retire from his job teaching sociology at Saint Joe's, and in fact was being pushed out. But around the time Selena moved back home (again), he began disappearing during work hours. It took him a month to admit he'd actually gone back into the classroom—at a fraction of his salary, even.

It was true Selena had been in the midst of a second stay in a psychiatric hospital during her mother's lavish retirement party, which had put a damper on those proceedings. Selena knew this because Alethia had later told her how "everyone," even Ms. Jenkins's "cute" son, had asked after her. "I had to tell him," Alethia had said, in an accusing tone, "that you were under the weather." But as far as Selena could see, her mother had not lied; she *had* been under the weather. She tried not to laugh at the thought of her mother trying to upsell Ms. Jenkins's whiny son, who would live at home forever because his mother made him hot breakfast every day and kept him in pocket money.

As far as Selena was concerned, she was fine. She had a longtime therapist (yes, her parents paid the bills), took her meds, and worked two jobs. Neither job was lucrative or offered much in the way of benefits, but her employers didn't expect too much or too little from her. She gave her parents just about all of both of her meager paychecks, setting aside SEPTA fare and student loan payments from two different schools. It was true that Selena's life was flying by in what seemed like a holding pattern, but she was stable and peaceful. There was nothing stopping her mother from living her paltry bourgeois dreams of leisure, but she suffered from near-physical pains at the memory of having said to Alethia, "I'm not stopping you from living out your paltry bourgeois dreams of leisure." It was one of the few memories that rose sharply from the muddle of those first few weeks out of the hospital. They were having lunch at a bright, soulless suburban cafeteria during an outing to buy new clothes for Selena's slimmer post-hospital figure.

Back then, in a level voice over a mostly untouched french dip sandwich, Alethia had asked, "Would you say you were a good daughter?"

I try, Selena thought now, standing in her mother's living room. *I do try.*

"Try what?" her mother asked, as she sat on the living room couch opening mail on the coffee table. On the TV a bailiff ordered the court to rise for a sassy Black judge.

"I was just . . ." Selena began, trailing off before she said, *remembering an earlier conversation and thinking about how I try to be a good daughter.* She pulled her hood off. "Hi, Mom. How are you doing?" This was the therapist's idea—using formality to create boundaries.

Alethia's eyes darted from Selena's raggedy sweatshirt to her face, as they always did. "I'm fine, thank you. Your friend called with some weird message for you."

"What?" Beneath layers of chemical stability, Selena felt an anxious rustling. What friend? There was a moon-faced white woman named Cady, who liked to come into the bakery to hide from her husband and small children. Or maybe this was her boss Scott pulling a weird phone prank. He might do a thing like that.

"Your old friend from college, from Bryn Mawr. The one whose husband just lost that election for state rep."

Selena froze.

Her mother addressed her again. "What's her name; it was so odd. I never knew how to spell it—Lysol?"

"Liselle," murmured Selena. It had been so brief and so long ago, somewhere between a memory and a fantasy. She knew it had happened, though, because if it hadn't then nothing had.

She moved past her mother, toward the ancient yellow wall phone in the kitchen. Her mother enjoyed talking on that phone to her sister and her best friend, in California, hating the distant sound of cordless phones, let alone cell phones, which she not-so-secretly thought had helped to drive Selena crazy (or at least crazier). As the judge on TV opined that any boy could make 'em but only a man could raise 'em, Selena gingerly touched the phone as if aliens had left it behind. On the notepad under it, her mother had written a telephone number and *Africa eat??*

Often when she returned from the bakery, Selena wanted to collapse by her mother's side in the living room, watching the daytime television parade of the angry and inarticulate. These court shows and talk shows made Alethia feel good about her own life; maybe they could do the same for Selena. But she knew if she sat down, she might not wake up in time for her night job.

Each afternoon when she came home from the bakery, she went straight to the kitchen, made peppermint tea, drank it, then took a nap, woke to an alarm, ate either spaghetti or grilled cheese, and headed out to her second job. This is what she'd learned from Dr. Greer, who, with her gray eyes, thick, shiny hair, and palpably sad air, was distractingly attractive for a non-TV therapist. "Just follow the routine," she had said. "It will support you like a spine."

Today the routine was upended by the phone call and Selena had trouble falling asleep. She had been thinking about Liselle on and off for nearly twenty years, sometimes frequently. She thought about her with longing, or rage, and wondered about the meaning of their time together. But it had been so long since they'd last been in touch. The fact that Liselle had called her, Selena, made her feel like she had made something in the cosmos happen with her own bent mind.

With unusual alacrity, she pulled herself up and went downstairs.

"Did you get some rest?" Alethia said.

"Not really."

"Want me to do something with your hair?"

Selena absently reached up to remember what she had done with her hair that day (or year) and verified a chunky ponytail.

She had cut off her dreadlocks after getting out of the hospital. In the month she'd been there that time, she hadn't tended to them at all. She had no memory of looking in the mirror in the room that always smelled of Windex vagina armpit. When she'd been discharged and looked at herself in her parents' bathroom, she'd actually looked crazy. Not melancholy, liberal arts educated crazy, but downtown-asking-in-a-high-voice-for-seventy-six-cents crazy. She'd planned to get her mother's sewing shears and hack off her dreadlocks, but she had floated about in a Klonopin fog for weeks. Her mother finally took her to the salon where her aunt Braxton styled hair, and while women in various states of perm and weave looked on in curiosity, horror, and irritability (knowing that Selena was not even on the schedule for that day), she had her hair shaved down to the scalp.

After that, Selena more or less ignored her hair, which grew out quickly, going from sad dyke to hopeful community librarian to religious shut-in. She washed, blow-dried, and combed it out once a week in a long but comforting ritual. She wore it in a puffy ponytail or two cornrows. It was neat and unstylish, that of a well-cared-for child. Sometimes she let her mother give her intricate braids, which Mrs. DaSilva liked to study. "Does that hurt?" she would ask, her withered, fuchsia-nailed hand shakily reaching closer to Selena's head. "It looks like it hurts."

"Sure, Mommy," said Selena. "I'll get the hair stuff."

She collected the comb, brush, and hair grease, and sat down on the rug in front of her mother. For a disorienting moment Selena felt like she was a little girl. Alethia switched channels and they watched Ellen DeGeneres in silence. Selena wondered if Ellen ever felt like she would die if she had to dance onstage one more time.

"So, what do you think she wants?" Alethia asked.

To be universally loved, Selena almost said, as she watched Ellen doing her incompetent moonwalk. She then realized her mother was asking about Liselle. It was irritating but not surprising; Selena relaxed into the familiarity of the combination, the gentleness of her mother's hands and the abrading quality of her questions. Alethia had always used these sessions to extract information, or pump it in. Selena never remembered this—until it was too late.

"I have no idea," she answered.

"Is this the first time you've talked to her since college?"

"Well, I didn't talk to her. You did."

"I can't believe she still has this telephone number after all this time. You haven't spoken to that girl in how many years?"

Selena shrugged but remained quiet. Neither of them had been *girls* for decades, and it would have been a useless provocation to attempt to explain to Alethia what she and Liselle had been to each other. Though she'd only called it a few times, Selena still knew the number to Verity's house, and she could probably dig up the New York number of Liselle's first cell phone. More numbers: Liselle was five foot seven; she had moved, in knowing Selena, from a size six to a size ten (approximately). Her birthday was June 5. Liselle had sent a postcard to Selena's parents' house several years ago with what Selena assumed was probably still her address: 5306 Lincoln Drive.

If Selena could remember all this, she knew Liselle could scare up her mother's number.

Alethia tried again. "What is 'Africa Eat'?"

"I don't know," lied Selena.

28

Selena's earliest memories of being human were from another world. Instead of being set in her parents' neat, unimaginative twin home in Wynnefield, she remembered being in Los Angeles in the Manhattan Beach condo of Alethia's best friend, Aunt Baby. Each year from age four to her teens, Alethia and Selena went, while Selena's father drank beer, smoked cigars, and played with model airplanes. Later Selena would wonder if that was really all he did while they were away.

Aunt Baby and Alethia had grown up together on a block that was now all but decimated, in North Philadelphia. "We made it out," Alethia would say. But the shrug belied the fact that by the time she was forty, the children they'd grown up with on that block were, to a one, dead, imprisoned, strung out on drugs, or scraping by in the margins. They were toothless men who drove trucks filled with scrap metal, dangerously fat women with missing teeth, raising grandchildren who'd come too early.

Alethia and Aunt Baby had graduated from the Philadelphia High School for Girls. Selena's mother had gotten two degrees from Temple University and worked as a school counselor. Aunt Baby, who had gone off to Penn State with a full scholarship, but dropped out in her second year, had forged her destiny in mysterious ways.

She had never "been a prostitute per se," Selena had once overheard her mother tell someone on the phone. Aunt Baby was a dazzling copper-colored woman with a large bosom, long legs, and naturally straight hair. She had a series of boyfriends that she called "investors."

"Surgeon's brain, that woman has," Alethia once told Selena as she cornrowed her hair in preparation for that year's visit. "Taught herself to read when she was three. But nobody ever really encouraged her to be what she could. See when you're that pretty, people don't want you to use your brain," she said, not seeming to consider that she was labeling Selena, twelve at the time, as "not that pretty."

Over the years, Aunt Baby had collected several houses in poor neighborhoods, both in Philadelphia and in Los Angeles, where she overcharged tenants. Selena came to associate the word "slumlord" with dazzling Black women. Aunt Baby herself lived in a condominium in a Black neighborhood near Beverly Hills that an old rich man ("the love of my life") had left her when he died. Aunt Baby had successfully fought off the claims of Mr. Barnes's children to the condo without paying a dime to a lawyer. It seemed to Selena that Aunt Baby *was* using her brains.

Each summer Selena and her mother spent a long weekend with Aunt Baby. Out in LA, they went to the beach, and ate Mexican food that was nothing like the gluey nachos at El Torito on City Line Avenue, sushi, which Alethia hated and Selena loved, and the only ribs Selena would eat, from a hole-in-the-wall in Compton. They went shopping at the Galleria, which made Philadelphia's Gallery mall seem like a multilevel public restroom. Alethia and Selena packed their best outfits for a yearly stroll down Rodeo Drive, doing their best to appear blasé as they stepped inside boutiques where, despite calmly hostile salespeople, Aunt Baby and Alethia tried on dresses and necklaces. In the evenings if they didn't eat out, Aunt Baby's longtime "Friend," a man named Mr. Maurice, would come around and grill steaks on the roof deck for the adults and hot dogs for Liselle.

Selena looked forward to these trips all year. The blue sky and warm air, day after day, made her think of God. She even loved Mr. Maurice, with his peaceful air, who asked after Alethia's foot and back problems, talked to Selena about her teachers, and seemed very attentive to Aunt Baby for a man with a wife and three children at home.

And then there was Aunt Baby, whose textures, looks, and spicy clove smell were like the center of a thick, soft quilt.

The dream always ended when they boarded the plane for the return trip from LAX and Selena's mother, to the alarm of the surrounding passengers, made her put on a paper surgical mask to protect her from the bad air of the cabin. During the dreary winter months, when she thought back on eating outdoors and the spectacle of weight lifters and skaters on the Venice Beach Boardwalk, the memories had the flavor of a dream.

The summer before she started high school, Selena overheard Aunt Baby, who was not really her aunt, and Mr. Maurice groaning, and the unmistakable sound of the bed squeaking.

Later that summer, at her first basement party when a boy held her close, she wanted to push him away and run. Instead, pretending she was Aunt Baby, she steeled herself, pushed back into him, and gave him her number. At the movies, on their first date, the boy, named Da'Mon, mentioned that he was in the process of breaking up with his girlfriend. Disappointed, she thought about Aunt Baby's moans, and still let him put his hand in her jeans in the theater as they watched a horror movie about space.

It would be years later, during one of Aunt Baby's rare visits to Philadelphia, when Selena first went into the hospital, that Selena would learn through a frank conversation in the Hades-like cafeteria that Aunt Baby had never cared for sex at all.

"It's just really not my thing," she said.

But what about that time I heard you? Selena wanted to ask. Of course, by then she had learned from her own life that women made noises; it was part of their job.

"Aunt Baby," Selena asked quietly, "have you ever slept with a woman?"

"Yes," said Aunt Baby. Then her mouth snapped shut. An image of Alethia, young, long-legged, smiling, passed before Selena's eyes. She'd never really looked at her mother, and it was too late to start.

29

It should not have, but it took Selena years to realize that before there was Liselle there was Paula. She'd appeared in Selena's homeroom on her first day at Central High. It turned out she had also been at middle school with Selena at Greenfield, but even though she had been sitting directly in front of her, Selena hadn't recognized her because she had shaved her head.

"Hey," the girl said, turning around in her seat.

"Oh, hey," Selena answered, trying to seem nonchalant, while peripherally scanning to see who was watching her talk to this freaky bald girl. Thankfully, the others seemed too absorbed in their own lonely freshman dramas.

"You were in Thompson's homeroom, right? Octave, right? Selena Octave."

"Uh, yeah."

Paula was a dark honey-colored girl. She'd had, Selena remembered, silky black hair down to her waist, and yet it had been said with awe that both her parents were Black. Now her head was a soft, boxy shape atop her skinny shoulders. Selena knew that Paula knew that Selena was thinking about her hair, and it made Selena unhappy to feel so transparent.

"That's what I thought," Paula said, and turned back around.

Selena looked at the downy hair at the nape of Paula's neck. *Cute,* she thought. Then she tried to unthink it.

Selena attempted to regain composure in gym class later that day. Considering how often she felt on the outside of things, she was embarrassed for acting like Paula was an alien. Between calisthenics she tried to make conversation.

"Did you have Grossman for English at Greenfield?" she asked.

"Yeah," said Paula. "He was actually cool. Anyway, I have a feeling that after a couple more days," she said, gesturing generally toward Central High, "we're really going to appreciate junior high."

"What do you mean?"

"'This is not your neighborhood school,'" Paula said, imitating their new principal. "'Look to the right and left of you.' What is this, Harvard? The building smells like a locker room full of cheese."

"It really does," Selena said, laughing with surprise.

While Paula studied Selena, who hoped she was passing muster with her fresh perm and her acid-washed jumper, the other kids were studying Paula. Here in the gym were some upperclassmen, boys and girls clumped in laughing groups. The boys looked over more than the girls.

"Who did you hang with at Greenfield?" asked Paula.

Selena shrugged. "Sometimes Maria Willow. Or Candice Jefferson." *Mostly no one,* she didn't say. It had always been that way. She drifted in and out of friendships that the other person never seemed to feel pressed to keep up. This happened because she could never say the things that were actually in her head. "What about you?" Selena asked, though she knew the answer. Paula and a boy named Lonny had been a thing since sixth grade. Selena, like most people, had been privy to much unkind commentary about how Lonny was dating Paula just for her hair. There had been furious speculation over whether they'd had sex.

"Mostly I just hung with Lonny," Paula said, shrugging.

"Are you still—?"

"Nope," said Paula. "Which is good 'cause there's some *decent* guys here."

Selena's heart sank for some reason. "Yeah, some of the upper-classmen are *decent*."

"Do you have a boyfriend?" asked Paula.

"Not really," said Selena, thinking of Da'Mon, who said they had to take it slow. He was apparently still in the protracted process of letting his girlfriend down easy. Selena didn't have the heart to tell him she didn't really care.

"'Not really,'" said Paula. "Look at you being all mysterious."

Selena said, "I'm not the one who came to high school with a witness protection haircut," and immediately wondered if that was too mean.

"I can't believe you said that," said Paula, her eyes seeming to grow wet. "I have cancer."

Selena shook with horror and began stuttering. This was record time, even for her, to make and lose a friend.

Paula giggled.

Before Liselle there was Paula, from whom Selena became inseparable, reminiscing about middle school, comparing favorite episodes of *A Different World*, Paula's obsession with the movie *Angel Heart* and her ensuing voodoo research; every Friday afternoon they hung out in Paula's room in a cloud of incense smoke, listening to rap music and appraising magazine pictures, talking about Central people whom they called Philistines for some reason. They sprawled on the little bed in a familiar way, trading secrets: Selena's experiments with sex, what Paula had done with Lonny.

One late-November afternoon, with dark falling fast, Paula revealed the truth of the haircut she'd gotten the summer before high school. She had become convinced that the same thing that attracted friends, made her a grandmothers' favorite, and hypnotized Lonny, was going to get her raped, killed, and dumped in an alley by one of the many grown men on the streets constantly hollering at her because of it. She told this to Selena, then did something like lurch at Selena, lips first.

Selena yelped. "No!"

"No, what?" said Paula.

"Were you about to kiss me?"

"Maybe," Paula said thoughtfully. "I thought you wanted to. I'm not going to force you or anything."

"Are you a lesbian?" asked Selena.

"Grow up, Selena." Paula rolled her eyes. "I just go with what I feel."

Before there was Liselle there was Paula, who shrugged and acted normal until the following Monday, when she began an elaborate freeze-out of Selena.

For her part, Selena had been basically prepared to live without friends in high school, but felt unprepared to lose this one. She went back over the moment again and again to try to fix it. *No, I did want to,* she wanted to scream at Paula. *I meant to!* her mind screamed every day, looking at the back of Paula's head in homeroom, while Paula chatted ostentatiously with Kim Beavers, a boring girl who sat next to her and decreed everything "nice," but in a Black way, like *noooooyyyce.*

Going into high school, Selena had steeled herself to continue battling the torment of her thoughts, but she had not been prepared to try to will her thoughts *back* to death squads in El Salvador and *away* from that afternoon in Paula's bedroom; she relived the moment every day, all day, each time saying yes in a different way. *Yes,* she moaned, shouted, whispered.

In springtime, toward the end of the year, Paula eventually began speaking to Selena again, saying hi in the halls. She wore a crown of short, sassy curls and was dating a junior, a player on the varsity basketball team. By then Selena told her parents she'd decided to transfer to Girls' High. Her father shrugged; he'd seen students from Central and Girls' both at Saint Joe's and they seemed the same to him. "Selena's not going to Saint Joe's," her mother snapped, aghast; she cited Central's higher test scores and more enriching enrichment programs. When Selena said ominously that she thought she would do better in a single-sex environment, she put a sharp staccato on the word "sex" and that ended the debate.

30

At the Philadelphia High School for Girls, Selena sat next to a reasonably friendly Black girl named Britain, who had the air of a busy but humble celebrity. At lunch, she attached herself to two best friends, Larissa and Queen. They were quiet, mainly communicating like plants, with occasional utterances about TV shows and the Power 99 countdown, and their respective church events. Their only edge seemed to be their shared hatred of a pretty, imperious upperclassman named Jill. There were girls at the school that Selena might have wanted to befriend, but they always seemed to be whispering in groups nearby, going quiet when Selena appeared. She wondered irrationally if they knew about her and Paula, or if they knew just about her.

After Da'Mon and the unconsummated heartbreak of Paula, there were other boys. They approached her at the bus stop, at the library, on the long walk from Girls' High to the Broad Street subway. They told her she was pretty for a dark-skinned girl and offered to walk with her down the hill. She wondered if they actually thought she was pretty (for a dark-skinned girl), or if she just seemed easy and lonely. Not that she cared.

She said goodbye to her virginity a few months before turning sixteen, with a football player from West Philadelphia High named Isaiah, who had large hands, big feet, and the smallest penis of the three she'd seen. (Later she felt like he treated her coldly for having seen it.) After Isaiah, she "went with" Edward, who said he wanted to wait until marriage but always wound up begging her to let him "poke it in." As she lay under these boys, she thought of Aunt Baby's golden, shapely legs stretching out from her torso, instead of her own dark bony ones; Aunt Baby's hair gently brushing her shoulders instead of hers, burned flat and sad in the "wrap" style against her scalp. She wondered if Aunt Baby had ever let anyone "poke it in." Selena thought she probably had.

"I hope," Alethia said to her one weeknight when Selena came home after her mother, "that you're keeping up with your homework."

"Yes," said Selena, who stood by her mother's side in the kitchen, flipping burgers in a skillet while her mother attacked potatoes with a masher. "I am."

"I also hope you're not getting a reputation. From my vantage point in schools, I know what that can do."

Just then the front door opened and Selena's father called out. Her mother shut her mouth grimly, but when they were alone she continued occasionally to speak in code ("I hope you're discreet; I hope you're protected"). Selena never explained to her mother that it was easy to be discreet when you barely talked to anyone, and that she couldn't have sex *without* a condom for her thoughts of HIV and the image of her own face covered in purple lesions.

Nor could she explain to her mother that the boys were the only thing she could do with her body to distract her brain from its journeys through hell.

One day, however, Selena found herself weary of quick after-school assignations and intrigue. She broke it off with Isaiah (and his friend Garrett) and let everything go quiet. In all the silence around her at school and at home, where her parents seemed to be experiencing a particularly brisk marital cold snap, she thought a lot about the homeless in downtown Philadelphia and the neglected children of drug addicts. When she got a TV for her sixteenth birthday, she began sleeping in its warm blue light; she dozed off amid the patrons of *Cheers*. She learned to set a timer so the television would not be on in the morning. The first time she woke to a dreary *M*A*S*H* rerun, it cast a pall over the entire day.

Despite her mother's haranguing about the importance of extracurriculars, Selena came straight home after school, arriving around 4:30. Her parents didn't usually turn up until after 6:00, though she knew from some tight-lipped comments of her mother's that her father, who worked professor's hours, could get home earlier and start dinner if he chose to do so. (He did not.)

The idea came from a scene in *The Godfather: Part II*. A minor character skips a cozy-looking dinner in federal prison to slit his wrists in a hot bath. Selena had seen the movie before, but watched with new interest.

"Does he do it in the bath so there's less cleanup?" she'd asked her father. He was a great fan of the *Godfather* movies, and of the idea of a laconic man who took on a familial burden and "kept his own counsel," despite the excellence of his consigliere.

"Well, I think in a hot bath, the blood comes faster," he said.

Though he saw the film every year, he looked entranced. Selena watched him watching it.

In the winter of junior year, her second year at Girls' High, she made a plan to come home, run a bath as hot as she could stand, get one of her father's razor blades, and cut her wrists. She thought about it every day (and thought and thought about it), because it stopped the world. She began to think of that time in the afternoon before her parents arrived as the Suicide Hours. That and her long commute, when she listened to Public Enemy on headphones, so loud it almost gave her a stomachache, were her favorite parts of the day.

One day her mother regarded her at dinner. "You seem upbeat. School going well?" Selena burst out laughing, which made her mother smile.

"Did you like high school?" she asked her.

"Sure," said her mother. "Of course. What's not to like? It was fun."

At this, Selena's father made a horsey sound. Alethia put her fork down. "Something to say, Carl? What? I didn't have fun in high school?"

"Speaking personally," he said, looking at Selena, "I found high school to be an inferno."

"You felt that way about college too. And then there was your first PhD program . . ."

"You just love telling me how I feel. Must be nice to know so much."

Selena never did answer the question of why she was feeling "upbeat." It continued to glow secretly in her.

One afternoon she realized she couldn't kill herself yet, because she had to write a note. The note was not to explain herself; she was not the point. The point was the continuing hell of the reservations, the squalid conditions, alcoholism, and poverty. She could write about what she saw in her tortured daydreams, what she'd read in books, and bequeath all her belongings, the ones that were still usable, including her almost-new TV, to a girl on a reservation. South Dakota came to mind. Maybe her parents could use her college fund to send that girl, who would be slender and serious, the color of adobe, to college.

Another afternoon, rereading the draft of her note, she realized she didn't need to talk about people thousands of miles away. What about the Richard Allen projects? She could leave her things to a girl there, a girl who had to traverse piss-smelling hallways and escape child molesters on elevators. A pretty Black girl who never got new clothes and was smarter than anyone thought she was.

Dissatisfied, Selena kept writing her drafts in a notebook with a purple floral pattern. Why, here in West Philadelphia there had been the MOVE fire. Of course, she could not leave anything to the children who'd died then, choking on smoke as they cried out for parents who roasted alongside them. (Had they held one another at the end?) She would address her note to Birdie Africa: "You have seen," she wrote, "the true face of the world."

One night as she did her physics homework with her back to the doorway of her room, she felt a presence. Wondering about ghosts, she turned to find her mother smiling. "Selena, please don't be angry with me, but I have to ask. What are you working on in English?"

Alethia came in and sat down on the bed. Selena, in a moment of panic, listened to her father downstairs groaning at a Flyers game. What kind of Black man watched hockey? Maybe one day they could discuss the fact that they were both weirdos.

"Mom, what are you talking about?"

"Well, it's just that you left your notebook open . . . I didn't look at it too closely, and I only read a page, but there was some incredible writing in there. Just heartbreaking."

Selena felt a chill, but her mother kept talking animatedly.

"I don't want to embarrass you, but seriously, the story about the girl in the projects, and Birdie Africa. They're really good. What is the project?"

"Well," said Selena, "it's not for English. It's a course called Writing for Publication. Those are just free writes." Selena was, in fact, enrolled in Writing for Publication, for which she wrote pallid poems about the colors of spring and a story about two white teenage girls having trouble with their friendship.

"I'm really glad to see you writing," her mother said. "It's wonderful that you finally found such a good outlet for your . . ." She trailed off. They had long stopped talking about the things Selena saw and worried about. Now they just pretended they had gone away.

"Did you show it to Dad?" Selena asked suddenly, knowing that her father would figure out what she was planning.

"I could if you want me to."

"No, I was just curious."

The next day, during the Suicide Hours, Selena looked back at her letter to Birdie Africa. She copied it over in her Writing for Publication notebook and decided to hand it in for her next project. She began to forget about the hot bath, though it was always there for her, a pretty dream when her parents snapped at each other or when Larissa and Queen addressed her coolly. She spent her afternoons adding drama and bigger words to her draft. She subconsciously plagiarized the last line of her MOVE story from the depressing Mildred D. Taylor book her mother had made her read. Hers went: "I cried for the others. The others and the house."

For Selena, who rarely got below an A, perhaps it should have been the case that getting a B plus on the assignment from Mrs. Wharton, complete with a comment that referred to MOVE as "filthy terrorists," jogged her back toward the original plan of killing herself. Certainly, it would have ruined Mrs. Wharton's year. But suicide started to seem embarrassingly dramatic, a B plus gesture. Not that she ever fully ruled it out.

31

ne chilly night in October, as they walked home from their feminist book group meeting, Liselle said, "We need a special word. Like a word for when one of us is about to punch somebody."

"Should the word be, like, a reminder to keep your thumb untucked? I learned that in self-defense. If you punch with a tucked thumb, you break your thumb."

"Yeah, the word could be, like, 'untuck,' Selena. Right." They fell into each other laughing.

A couple of other girls who had been in the meeting fell into step next to them. "Hey, Belmont, what are you guys conspiring about?" the one named Mae asked. Selena was reminded of something Liselle had told her, that it seemed to upset white girls when the two of them spent too much time together in public. Behind their smiles was always an air of jealous surveillance.

"Oh, you know," said Liselle. "Our ten-point program."

"Well, you guys can take the slow boat if you want. Come on," she said to the droopy girl beside her. "I gotta get indoors and *warm my ass*. It is as cold as *a bitch out here!*"

"But then why is she wearing Birkenstocks?" Liselle murmured. Selena wore a sly expression. "You know she called me twice after the last meeting? 'Just to chat'? She never got around to it, but I think she wanted to ask me out."

"You didn't tell me that," Liselle said, trying not to feel strange. "How did you feel about that?"

"Deeply uninterested."

"So, as I was saying," Liselle continued, "we need something we can say that's basically for each other that's like, *I'm about to blow this shit up and I'm taking all of these white bitches*—I shouldn't say 'bitch.'"

"I won't tell," said Selena.

"Do you know when that girl Connor started coming to this book group last year, she was dating some Black basketball player from Temple?"

"Well, as you may recall, last year I was still in high school—"

"Anyway, now she's what? Talking about how we can't read Frantz Fanon in the group because no men?"

"Well it *is* a *feminist* book group," Selena said mildly.

"Are you taking her side?"

"No, I think she's wack as hell. Anyway, now that you told me about the basketball player, I get why she insisted we read *The Autobiography of Malcolm X*—talk about where is the feminism?—and tried to make the whole discussion about his treatment of his white girlfriend."

"Yeah, she felt like she was *Laura* and that basketball player who played her was Malcolm X."

"Malcolm X was very tall," Selena said.

"You are a fool."

Without having discussed it, they were at Liselle's, where they went every night unless Selena's roommate was out of town. Once, they had made the mistake of coming back to Selena's room on a Friday night. Mary Frances had been excited by plans to catch a ride to a Villanova party to be with her people, some other white girls looking to get drunk and lightly felt up. But just as Selena had stopped talking about the U.S. government and Nicaraguan death squads long enough to let Liselle touch her, Mary Frances had burst into the room weeping.

"What's our word?" asked Liselle, Selena's head on her lap. "Because I think punching Mae in the face would get me kicked out before graduation."

Selena sat up, rifled through her backpack, and fished out the copy of *Zami* she'd borrowed from Liselle. "What about 'Afrekete'?"

"You're so corny," Liselle said flatly. Selena knew she was reliving the trauma of the B minus, after which she'd declared Professor Bruin "dead to me," but hadn't stopped quoting her lectures. Liselle had been excited to tell Selena what Professor Bruin had told them about the writer Jessie Redmon Fauset, a Girls' High alum, who had been accepted to Bryn Mawr only to be driven off the campus when the president of the college discovered that she was Black.

"You're not going to call me corny when you hear this mix I made you," Selena said, still going through her things.

"I will if it's corny."

"Bite me," said Selena evenly. She retrieved a sticker-decorated cassette, got up, and put it into the boom box resting on a milk crate. She stood and pantomimed a microphone and made a pained R&B singing face: *So, you're having my baby and it means so much to me . . .*

"Is that 'Forever My Lady'? What the hell?"

Selena held out her hand, as if to invite Liselle to dance. "What did they call it in *Zami*? A 'slow fish'? You have to admit this is the best song ever made."

"On what grounds?"

"Listen to that keyboard solo. This can be our song."

"I don't know about that," said Liselle, feeling silly as they swayed together. She'd suffered through the song at a few awkward basement parties where she'd either not been asked to dance or been crushed up against a sweaty boy smelling of vodka and aftershave, using her to polish his erection.

Just as the song was about to end, Selena broke away and moved back over to the stereo. "I'm playing that again. I'm playing it until you love it."

◎◎ **32** ◎◎

They never said, "I love you."

hat happened to your friend?" said Mary Frances one morning after winter break, as she and Selena trudged through the snow to breakfast. "You guys were so cute together. What was her name? Liesl?"

Selena thought ruefully of the fun she and Liselle had enjoyed at Mary Frances's expense. Another first! Complimenting a lesbian couple! What would they think back in Ohio?

"*Liesl* was a character in *The Sound of Music*. It's Li*selle*," she said, laughing, though her chest stung with longing. "I don't know," said Selena. "I think maybe we're not good at relationships. Not just the two of us together, but separately, neither of us. It got kind of crazy." For years after, Selena felt deeply ashamed of the violent moment they'd shared at the end, but there was only one person she wanted to talk about it with, and, sadly, that was Liselle.

"You're so lucky you're both girls. At least you speak the same language. This guy Scooter from Haverford, sometimes I feel like he literally can't understand English when I say, like, 'Call me later.'"

Selena laughed. "Scooter's just not very conscientious. I'm sure his English comprehension is fine and I'm sure he likes you." In fact,

Selena was sure of neither. "You know," she said, changing the sub-ject, "I don't think anyone's ever been called lucky for being gay." As they entered the cafeteria, the muddled smell of oversweet muffins and disinfectant hit them. The months had conditioned Selena to feel hunger as a response to these questionable aromas.

"But I mean, there's so many things lesbians don't have to deal with."

Selena cut off the speech that was coming by asking her where they should sit. Though she did sometimes feel a prurient interest in Mary Frances's intimate life, she knew it was better not to get involved. (Which is perhaps why she was utterly taken aback when Mary Frances began "living as a man" after college.)

After they had trays and sat down, Selena scanned the room for Liselle. As always, she was both relieved and sad not to see her. She did, however, see Liselle's ex Kit, her head covered by a black wool cap, slumped over a bowl.

"I mean, of course, I guess there are a lot of bad things gay people have to deal with, especially men," said Mary Frances, col-oring. Selena looked back at Kit. Now that another girl had joined her, she pulled off her cap and revealed a head of cropped red curls. The girls smiled at each other.

"It's okay," she told Mary Frances. "Nothing makes sense."

Selena had cried between classes for two days and spent the win-ter holidays in a fog. "Are you still writing?" her mother had asked hopefully. Selena had entertained fond thoughts of the Suicide Hours, but her parents were constantly underfoot, being too friendly. She came back to campus four days early to be alone in her room, so she could cry and masturbate in peace.

She went to class, wrote essays, cataloged and shelved at her library work-study job. Trying not to think about their dates in Liselle's suite, she watched *The Oprah Winfrey Show* alone in the common room, abruptly turning off an episode dedicated to finding lost loves. They'd been together barely four months, she kept reminding herself, and college was not the real world; it was like sleepaway camp. She skated on the ice of the despair, trying not to break through. Her dorm did not have a bathtub.

34

I t must be so amazing to live in New York," Selena said in 1996, adjusting her tank top, which she knew sometimes slipped askew. She noted Liselle's furtive glances at her cleavage, which made up for the catcalls she'd had to endure on the way. "Gimme a lick!" one man had yelled, blasting "Ice Cream" out of his car. When Selena looked at him, he'd been surprisingly elderly, with handicapped plates. *Probably his wife's,* she'd thought.

It had been a little over a year since Liselle had graduated from Bryn Mawr and Selena had been hospitalized for the first time. Finally beginning to feel normal, but also restless and lonely, Selena reached out. Liselle was living in New York, she was told by the Wicked Witch of West Philly, Verity. To Selena's surprise, Liselle had gotten in touch with her during a weekend trip back home.

The women sat over syrupy whipped cream concoctions at the fancy new coffee shop, Starbucks, in downtown Philadelphia. Liselle seemed disappointed with her life. This irked the shit out of Selena, though she tried not to show it. She had faced herself in the mirror of her childhood bedroom before the meeting. "Be positive," she'd said. "Be sunny," she'd warned. "Be sexy."

Now she tried to sound curious about Liselle's life and keep the edge out of her voice. She did not point out that some people did not see what they had, or that some people were stuck finishing their degree at Temple and living with their unhappy parents, while the fortunate were living on the Upper East Side, working like proper adults. Instead she said, "Tell me one awesome thing."

Liselle rolled her eyes. "Once, I went out dancing with my roommates and when I was coming home late, a limo pulled up and the driver offered us a ride for the price of a cab and told us that he had just dropped off LL Cool J."

"So, you got to ride in a limo?"

"What sex plantation would that car have taken us to? No, I'm just giving you a sense of the kind of things that happen in my glamorous new life."

"What about your job? 'Editorial specialist' sounds so official."

"I put magazine articles, mainly recipes nobody wants, on the World Wide Web. I don't have health insurance."

"Where can I go to read the articles?"

"Do you need a recipe for white chocolate meringues?"

Selena's exaggerated expression of horror brought a smile to Liselle's face. "So does that pay a lot? Posting recipes online that nobody wants to cook?"

"You can be sure that it doesn't. I'm thinking I might get into teaching."

Selena knew Liselle had said "coffee" instead of "dinner" because she wanted this to be a calm, platonic meeting. But Selena had also calculated that though they were two grown women with no place to go for privacy, her parents would be at work during the coffee, which Selena had nudged earlier to give them more time. Just in case. She put an inspirational hand on Liselle's thigh. "You should do it. You would be an awesome teacher."

Liselle looked at Selena's hand, but she didn't move it. "I guess. I mean, I'm not going to be an anthropologist or a writer or . . ."

"Or what?"

"Forget it. Teaching just seems like something I could do. What are you up to?"

As casually as she could, Selena started talking as she took a pill. There were five of them throughout the day.

"I'm starting a summer internship next week," she said, wondering how she was going to deal with the pill routine at her office. "It's at this place called the Women's Alliance. They basically give out money to women who can't afford abortions."

"That's kind of deep."

"I mean, it really helps a lot of desperate women. The hard part of the job is that apparently they get, like, thirty desperate calls a day, but can only give money for ten. And then I'm the only person in the office besides the director."

"For your sake, I hope she's cool."

Now it was Selena's turn to shrug. "She's okay." Of course, there was something off about the woman. For ten years, she had been working alone in an office where she gave strangers money to get abortions. But who was Selena to judge? And anyway, she wanted to keep this interaction breezy and pleasurable. Then maybe Liselle would invite Selena to visit New York. Maybe once she got up there, they could pick up where they'd left off—before it had gotten bad. Selena's heart raced with sugar, caffeine, and love.

"A DJ," said Liselle suddenly, as they used their straws to poke the gritty slush of their drinks. "That's what I really want to be when I grow up."

"What?"

"Remember that night—?"

"Of course," said Selena. "Of course I remember. Anyway, you'd be awesome, of course. What would your DJ name be?"

"I haven't thought about it."

"DJ Lorde?" said Selena. "Like Audre. But only those in the know will know." She winked.

Liselle looked pleased, but then she took Selena's hand off her thigh and squeezed it. "I want to know what it's really been like," she said.

Selena knew then that they could never stay light.

35

The first time Selena was in the psychiatric hospital, she tried not to think about Liselle, because the memories made the area around her ribs hurt. When she could, she trained her thoughts on the idea of sanity. Other times they ranged over space and time or back to hazy moments: her father finding her at home playing with a knife, a long walk from Wynnefield to Aunt Braxton's, where she'd turned up with one shoe.

The second time Selena was in the hospital, she clung to memories of Liselle, though she had not seen her in years. She told herself that if she could remember Liselle, her clay smell, the way she covered her mouth when she laughed, then she'd survive the slow-motion nightmare of the institution. She was also comforted by the fact of who she herself had been back then. A student. A girlfriend.

Selena's romantic life before and after hospital stays was a series of stands: one night, two weeks, two months at most, three women, two men; one had accompanied his girlfriend to the Women's Alliance for an abortion voucher. When the woman, who was feeling nauseated, was in the restroom, he slipped Selena his number.

Weeks later, as the man solemnly kissed different parts of her body in his underfurnished apartment with its massive television, Selena laughed suddenly, thinking of Liselle as "the Wolf."

In truth, Selena had occasionally faked orgasms with Liselle to get to the spooning.

"What you laughing at?" asked the boyfriend of the woman, smiling. "You won't be laughing in a minute."

"Mmm," she said, and tried to seem serious, but she almost laughed again when he orgasmed and called out his own name. She thought, *It would have been hilarious, if he hadn't just fucked me.*

36

What were you doing before this?" asked Selena's supervisor Scott. If he was in the building after her cleaning shift, he liked to chat. When she came to his tiny back office to clock out, he sometimes offered her a little paper cup of brown liquor. She had seen such a thing only on TV before this, lawyers celebrating a courtroom victory, for instance. She wasn't even really sure what he put in the cup.

"Didn't I put that on my application?"

He shrugged. "I mean, I just glanced at it to make sure you weren't a criminal. Which I could tell by looking at you. I could tell you were like me: a 3-D Black person trying to fit into a 2-D box."

Selena, who had once been booked for disturbing the peace in the same Starbucks where she'd once met up with Liselle, let it pass. All she'd done (that she remembered) was pour milk on the floor, screaming about the poison of whiteness. No one had been hurt. Her record had been expunged.

"I worked on and off at the Women's Alliance before this," she answered.

Scott chuckled. "You say that like everyone knows what it is."

Selena remembered how cagey she'd had to be with her parents about the job, even though she was just an intern and living with them when she had first taken it. They were pro-choice in theory, and as a high school counselor, Alethia, in particular, could not really afford to take any other attitude. But her father harbored deep suspicions about Black fertility and white medical facilities. So it had felt unseemly explaining to her parents that while she would not actually be inserting hoses in vaginas, she was handing out money to end pregnancies. She never quite told them what she did and they never quite knew.

Selena experienced Scott's shocked eyes as a thrill as she said, "I helped women get abortions. The organization had a certain amount of money per day, per week, per month, and I had to decide who got to use it."

"Okay," he said. "Okay."

She looked at him wryly. "Is it okay?"

"Whiskey?" he asked. He'd been holding the cup as he spoke and Selena had been debating whether to accept it. Alcohol was contraindicated with her daily pill regimen, but on the nights when she accepted the cup from Scott, she tended to sleep better. Of course, the mornings after were especially terrible, but you couldn't have everything. Selena perched on the edge of the saggy plaid love seat in his office and took a sip. He sat down across from her, at his desk. She felt the drink burn going down.

"I know," he said. "This is just the work juice. I keep the good stuff at home. One of my buddies from school gave me a thirty-year-old bottle from Scotland. Maybe you can come by the house and sample it one day."

Selena blinked at him. She thought about the fact that the office was located in the basement of a hulking building that was nearly empty. She remembered again that Liselle had called her, and thought about how Liselle had once accused her of never being afraid of anything real. For her part, Liselle had been terrified of winding up like her mother: someone who worked hard, lived alone, and barely held on. Selena had said Verity seemed fine; hers was not a fate to fear.

Selena knew she should have been afraid of Scott, but in that moment, she became aware that she was not much afraid anymore. Except, perhaps, of loneliness.

"So, was that a hard job?" Scott asked, seeming to realize that the subject of sampling whiskey at his house was a non-starter. He reclined in his chair and put his feet up.

"It was the best job I've ever had, or at least my favorite."

Selena thought of the Women's Alliance, the small, bright, orderly office, and of Kendra, a sleekly dressed white woman from Olney with a sculpted Black woman's hairstyle. Selena had loved the job, but kept trying to quit to go somewhere bigger, fancier, something that seemed more secure. She confided in Kendra that she had interviewed for an entry-level job at Planned Parenthood, but Kendra had convinced her that the Women's Alliance needed her more. "I mean, yeah, you can serve Catholic school girls who can't tell their parents they're having sex," she had said dismissively over drinks at the Caribou Café.

Selena did quit and spent almost three years working a purely secretarial job at a big nonprofit foundation that funded the art forms most fervently cherished by rich white senior citizens. The salary allowed her to finally leave her parents' house and get a nice apartment downtown, but gave her days a certain numbness. Almost every day at that job, as she sat at her large desk at the switchboard, different parts of her fell asleep. She worried she had circulation problems, but a doctor confirmed that the problem was severe ennui. One day Kendra called her and said she'd landed a big grant and could match Selena's foundation salary.

"Helping women get abortions was your favorite job?" said Scott. Selena remembered the pleasurably exhausted feeling she'd had after a day of frantic calls. Most of the women and girls had seemed grateful; some dazed. Some of them acted irritably entitled in a way that Selena recognized as the lack of self-awareness she had only ever witnessed among one other group of people: the rich. But most important, the job had not hurt Selena. The women's distressing circumstances, their degradation: it had not really bothered her, not even the dull-sounding teenage girl who'd said she'd been raped by her stepfather. Selena had set that girl up with an appointment at Planned Parenthood and two counselors. It had made her feel purposeful.

"Do you know that you're a bitch?" one woman had said when Selena turned her down for a voucher and only offered to connect her with counseling. Kendra said they'd worked with this woman too many times already, that they were trapped in her cycle, and that they needed to help somebody else, to which the woman said, "Well, how about I help myself by coming to kick your little white ass." In another life Selena would have been terrified, but she'd learned to identify the sound of the woman's erratic speech rhythms as *high*. She had met women like this in the hospital. They had not kicked her ass and neither would this voice on the phone. She had almost laughed at the woman; instead, she slowly recited the number of a drug treatment facility and hung up.

"Should I prefer cleaning an office building at night?"

"I guess not, but did you feel like you had the right to play God like that? Wasn't it weird to you that you could make one person's future not happen at all?"

"Well, how did you feel when you fired that woman Alisa last week? The pregnant one who already had three kids? Those are actual people whose lives you're messing with, not clumps of cells."

"Damn. Poor Alisa. She needs help. Maybe you should tell her about the Females' Alliance or whatever." Then he had a thought. "Why did you leave that job?"

Selena sighed. "The director was stealing, so the funders pulled out." One day she'd come in and a dour, aggressively drab white woman had been there, the opposite of Kendra with her bright peplum dresses and her Italian horn of plenty necklace. "Kendra is not coming," the woman had said. When the job ended two weeks later, after extensive interviews and depositions, Selena started miserably temping, looking for something permanent, as the economy fell apart. One night she called Liselle's mother's house. *She's married*, Verity had barked. Things started slipping for her.

"But you could get another job like that, right? You went to college," said Scott. "My fiancée works for an education nonprofit."

"Scott," Selena said, "is your fiancée going to give me a job?"

"I mean, I guess not."

"I better get going then." Selena had drained her cup but was surprised to find that it was more difficult than usual for her to get out of the depths of the saggy couch.

"Selena, Selena," Scott sang, "where are you always *going*?"

"Are you okay, Scott? How many little cups did you have?"

He slammed his fist on his desk. "I'm not okay at all. I demand to know where you're going."

"Home."

"That's your parents' house. That's not your home. Come with me. Let's run off somewhere. Let's go to Greece."

"What's in Greece?"

"We could be Black gods there. Do you know that the Greek gods were all imitations of the Egyptian ones?"

Scott was not tall. He was compact but also looked sturdy. He had gotten up from behind his desk and was standing over her. He was sallow-skinned with a patchy beard and not attractive in the least. But Selena thought he had a kind look.

"Scott, are you going to kill me?"

"No!" he shouted.

"Are you going to rape me?"

He paused. "Definitely not."

"Are you going to fire me?"

"Why would I do that?"

"Okay. Then can you walk me to the bus stop?"

"Maybe. I mean, I have to get all the way back to Mt. Airy. I guess I can't drive," he said sadly. "I can't believe I did this shit again. Odetta is gonna fuck me up."

"Did you say Mt. Airy?" asked Selena. She thought of the notepad at her mother's house. *Afrekete.* That's what she herself should have said when she called Liselle's house the last time, when she was falling into a hole. *Afrekete.* Or when she learned from a flyer in the bookstore that a Black woman named Gloria Joseph had been Audre Lorde's partner in the years before—and right up until her death.

"What of it?"

"I'll go up there with you. To Mt. Airy. There is somebody." She suspected the liquor was flowing in her blood, shaping her to its will. "Somebody I need to see."

37

The first time Liselle had seen him, he'd been on the outer edges of the crowd at a fundraiser at the Senegalese restaurant on Germantown Avenue. The sight of him gave her a chill, but not because she had any idea who he was or what it would mean.

Winn had been in the tiny back room going over comments with the image consultant Ivelisse Peña, which seemed unnecessary to Liselle for something so informal. But Ron kept saying, "Leave nothing to chance," which is also why they had left Patrice at home. First he'd said he wouldn't go and when they insisted, he'd come home with green dreadlocks. Liselle had been briefly afraid that Winn might hit him. "Are you *really* fucking with me like this?" he had yelled. It reminded her ruefully of the last time she'd almost done violence to someone she loved.

It was Liselle's job to mingle. Despite her fantasies of being a public figure, Liselle had never had Verity's easy ways with regular Black folks. First she had been shy, then she'd been a lesbian. Now she lived in a big house in Mt. Airy with Winn, and spent most of her time with white people and Patrice. And yet, during the campaign it was partly her job to convince Black people (and the post-hippie neighborhood old-timers of all races) that Winn was not the gentrification candidate. That he was *not* the candidate of white people who had returned to the city eager to resume the reins of governing as their due. Anyone would be right to be skeptical of her spiel. She told herself, though, that at least her and Patrice's fortunes were tied to Winn's. It wasn't *just* a vote for some entitled white man.

When she spotted William McMichael, she was feeling stranded between tables, looking for friendly faces. She'd barely had time to approach an older light-skinned couple. "I'm Liselle Belmont, Winn's wife," she'd said. The woman said, "We will need a table for two." As Liselle explained that she was not a waitress and they'd have to find dinner elsewhere, McMichael moved toward her from the edges of the crowd. After the couple walked away from Liselle and out of the restaurant, he was in front of her and there was nowhere to go.

In her late thirties, Liselle had begun to entertain the small, nagging worry that something would destroy her home, or at least unsettle it. She had imagined a female presence, young and reckless. Someone who appreciated things about Liselle that Winn had never even noticed. As she looked at this heart-stoppingly Black and smooth-faced man, a sense of doom rose in her throat. Everything he wore, his pearl-gray suit, open-necked white shirt, looked crisp, almost to the point of being bespoke. His loafers glowed even in the restaurant's dim lighting. She stuck out her hand and tried to summon something like charm.

"Thanks for coming out. I'm Liselle Belmont."

"William McMichael. Pleased to meet you."

"I'm Winn's"—she did not mean to pause—"wife."

"Nice," he said.

Nice?

"So how did you hear about Winn's campaign?"

"Some of my more politically involved friends," he said.

"I guess they'd have to be." Liselle laughed. "It's not a flashy race, though it is an important one."

"I hear that," he said. She heard it, too, heard herself saying it with conviction and was impressed, since she wasn't at all sure it was true. She had learned at some point during the race that there were 435 members of the U.S. House of Representatives and wondered about how each one of them contributed to shaping her reality. Though it made her feel treacherous, she occasionally wondered if Church Williams had a hand in maintaining the normalcy of her life in some unclear way that the inexperienced Winn might disrupt.

"So what's the pitch?" he asked. "Why should we turn our back on Church Williams after his fifteen years of service? I am, of course, understanding that you have a particular stake in the outcome of the race."

"Do I, though?" Liselle laughed in order to stall. She was not warmed up enough to give her prepared "offhand" comments. She cleared her throat. "I think Church Williams has served this community to the best and the limits of his ability. But at this point it's possible the community serves *him* more. I think, well, I know, that Winn will bring new energy both to old problems and to new challenges."

"For example?" He wore an amused look.

According to Ivelisse, Liselle was *never* to speak in specific terms that could be quoted later, but stick to broad themes highlighting the idea that Winn was the future and Church was the past. But talking to this fine Black man made her feel vain about her intelligence.

"Well, for one thing, the neighborhood is swarming with developers, none of whom have the neighborhood's best interests at heart. For another thing, Church Williams is reputedly such a strong advocate for education, but that is nowhere in evidence in our community's failing schools—"

"But how much control does a rep have over something local and fine-grained like that?"

"We will find out when we have somebody more committed to change, I guess."

"How does gentrification fit into this for Winn?"

"New residents, new interests . . ." Liselle knew she had to stop there. She had said too much already.

"Meaning?"

"Excuse me for fumbling this a bit. I'm new to this. As you can see, I'm not the typical political wife."

He shrugged. "Who is?"

"Laura Bush?"

"You're not Laura Bush?"

Suddenly Ron Mack was at her side. "Liselle, I need you. A guy from the *Chestnut Hill Local* wants a quote from the family. Excuse me," he said to William McMichael. "I hope Winn has your support. I need to borrow this lovely lady for a moment."

"Of course." He nodded, making a gallant gesture with his hand.

"It was really nice to meet you," Liselle said. "I hope you like what you hear tonight." She was proud of herself for improvising that.

"No doubt," he said.

"Who was that?" asked Ron, as the man moved through the crowding room, which wasn't that big to begin with. She saw now that it had been a clever strategy to hold it there. It made the event seem successful even if it wasn't.

"A constituent?"

Ron looked wary. "You all seemed to be getting on. Nice work."

That night when Winn spoke, she was embarrassed that Winn was repeating the lines she'd spouted to the man earlier. "New energy to old problems . . . new energy to new problems . . . background in real estate law . . . new residents, new housing challenges. Doing right by old residents and new . . . schools . . . time for change . . ." Since 2008, every candidate had been shouting "change." Liselle wondered what rallying cry would come after that.

Winn dabbed at himself with a tissue she hoped wouldn't disintegrate on his face. He looked confident and happy and she remembered him back at Media Inc. meetings, interjecting as the other assistants remained silent. (*Oppose busing.* She laughed.) The Black half of the crowd nodded encouragingly while others listened politely. Later, Liselle would not dampen his excitement about that particular detail by telling him what every Black person knows: *We are among the most polite members of humanity.*

William McMichael came to say goodbye as she and Winn were posing for a picture.

"Laura," he said.

She felt it in her knees.

"Who was that?" asked Winn without breaking his mask of a smile. An overdressed young woman who reeked of perfume snapped their picture for social media.

38

The second time, she saw him in the café on Germantown Avenue where she spent most mornings.

Though she was on leave from teaching, purportedly to help with the campaign, Winn had come home late one evening from an "emergency" strategy meeting to tell her she was no longer needed. She knew it was because she was awkward. She could scarcely bring herself to shake indiscriminate hands during flu season, or smile on command. Lacking those skills, even as a Black woman, she was actually holding him back with Black voters. Without her there, Winn could traffic in the particular mystique of a white man married to a Black woman. White *plus*, like Robert De Niro. And then of course there was a small but significant voting constituency bordering the Northeast, close to Ron's favorite steak shop. Those people didn't want to see her or Patrice no matter what.

Now her role was to host the occasional dinner for friends of the campaign, and she edged closer to becoming one of Verity's worst slurs—a "house-fucking-wife." Sometimes she wondered if she'd ever see William McMichael again.

She usually frequented the coffee shop to drink espresso concoctions and read novels between Sisyphean household errands, but this morning was different. She'd brought with her a pretty yellow notebook that she'd picked up on impulse in the bookstore. She often bought little notebooks in which she kept track of shopping lists and important dates, planning for Patrice, but she knew this notebook was not for that.

Today Liselle had come to the coffee shop with an idea that had seized her in the early morning hours. She was going to write down her memories of Selena: all of them. She knew that was why she'd bought this particular notebook. She wasn't sure why she was thinking about her so much but she felt like the memories were a message or a riddle she would figure out if she wrote down what she remembered. She had eaten half her bagel and was down to the dregs of her coffee, but feared the task at hand. Finally, she opened the notebook and began to describe Professor Bruin's class. And then she saw him.

He was sitting across the room on the uncomfortable couch near the fake fireplace. Her breath caught in her chest. She looked down at her page. When she looked up again, he was in front of her.

"Hello, Liselle."

"Hello?" she said lightly, closing the book, trying to suggest she wasn't sure who he was. But then she knocked her (mercifully) empty coffee cup with her elbow.

"Let me get that," he said. There was a kerfuffle as they both reached for it.

"Do you remember we met at a fundraiser for Winn's campaign?" he asked, righting the cup.

"At the restaurant, right? Seems like decades ago," she said, which was true in the sense of the many phases of the campaign, but false in that she felt it had been only days since she'd met him.

"Mind if I sit?" he asked, handing her a business card. She froze reading it. Before she could answer, he was sitting across from her.

"FBI?" she stammered.

"Can I get you another coffee?" he asked.

"I don't let the FBI buy me drinks."

He laughed. "I'm not the FBI."

"You're the only FBI I know. How did you know I'd be here?" she asked, grateful for the din of the shop. Dreadful folk-pop came through the store's speaker system while two skinny flat-haired girls shrieked in affirmation across the room. Nearby a man was flexing his status on a work call and an elderly woman wearing a thick layer of makeup rustled a stack of several newspapers.

"Liselle," he said in a low voice, brushing away her question, "I wanted to ask you about some of the people your husband's been talking to in connection with his campaign."

She pulled herself up straighter. "He talks to a lot of people and kisses a lot of strange babies. That's what a campaign is. Well, people don't actually let you kiss their babies anymore. Do I need a lawyer for this conversation?"

"I don't think so. This is just a conversation in a coffee shop. Between two . . . people."

He reclined and it was slightly sexy, which made her angry.

"Let's back up," he said. "I work on the outskirts of the political process to be sure there are no irregularities in terms of fundraising and vote soliciting. There are a number of people who hover around Philadelphia politics that we're keeping an eye on. I'm wondering if Winn has run into any of them."

"Is Ron Mack one of the people?" Liselle knew that Winn, who was simultaneously the most gregarious and most secretive person she'd known, would have killed her for mentioning Ron, who'd brought him into this and had become his shadow.

"What do you know about Ron Mack?" asked William Mc-Michael, but his face betrayed nothing.

"I don't know. I guess he gets involved in a lot of political races and lives in Chestnut Hill. His daughters used to compete at the Devon Horse Show."

"Well," he said, squinting. "I mean, we already know about the Devon Horse Show. We're all over that."

She did not want to, but she laughed.

"You're a Philly girl, right?" he asked.

"Girl?" she said with raised eyebrows, not because it belittled her, but because it did not sound like him.

"My bad."

"Yes, I'm from Philadelphia. Where are you from?" She didn't know why she was making conversation, but was interested in his answer.

"Chocolate City," he said. "Southeast. You know anything about DC?"

She knew it had been a long time since she'd heard anyone call it "Chocolate City," and it made him less cute, like saying "Frisco." "I mean, I've been there, obviously. I remember really liking the Frederick Douglass house."

"In Anacostia. I like it there too. I wonder what Frederick Douglass would think of America now," he said pensively.

"I mean, he would definitely work for the FBI, right?"

"Right. So, I'm just trying to connect some dots. You're local, your husband is not. Did you introduce him to anyone important to the campaign? I know that your mother has worked for the city for a number of years in the Department of Licenses and Inspections."

"My mother?" Liselle laughed nastily. "Where are you getting this hot intel? She cares more about the cancellation of *All My Children* than about Winn's campaign."

"Noted. As I told you, I'm just trying to map some connections."

"Look, Mr. McMichael, can I ask you, respectfully, if Winn did something wrong?"

"I haven't asked you anything about Winn," he said, which was true.

She pressed. "Did *I* do something wrong?"

"Did you?" he asked.

"Not that I know of."

"Okay, then."

"Mr. McMichael?" she said, her voice cracking.

"Please call me William."

Just then, the old white woman in the heavy-looking velvet dress approached their table. She leaned in slowly and Liselle saw that her blue eyes were bleary. "I just have to tell you two that you make the most beautiful couple."

"We—" began Liselle.

"Thank you," said William McMichael.

"Have a wonderful day," said the woman, grinning at nothing on her way out of the coffee shop. Liselle noticed she'd left a messy pile of her papers and coffee things on her table, blissfully oblivious to the trash bins and trays helpfully positioned at the door.

"What a time to be alive," he said.

"So," said Liselle, "how does somebody like *you* end up working in this, er, field?"

"How does anybody wind up at any job? Interest, skills, timing. I have a question for you. How does somebody like *you* wind up married to somebody like Winn Anderson?"

"In what sense?"

"Can I be frank?"

"At your own risk."

"Well, it seems like you'd have run in very different circles. And you just seem . . . a bit, well, I don't want to say—out of his league?"

"I'm going to stop you right there," said Liselle, biting back a smile. "What are your other questions?"

They chatted for over an hour, some about Liselle's background, mostly about the campaign. He tossed countless dry male names she didn't know at her and she quickly forgot them. Then they talked about his work in Philadelphia and a counterfeit luxury goods ring he'd helped break up. Before he left the coffee shop, he lightly suggested that Liselle might not want to alarm Winn with news of their meeting.

39

Pain shot through the back of Liselle's head. Opening her eyes, she was surprised by the sight of Xochitl standing over her saying, for the first time, maybe, her actual first name. Liselle was hit by a wave of emotion for Jimena's daughter, her smooth brown face and beaked nose.

"I'm okay," Liselle said finally, though her ankle vibrated with pain.

"Should I call an ambulance?" Liza yelled.

"No!" Winn said sharply, and Liselle remembered that she'd finally told him. Now he was afraid of anyone coming in from outside. He reached down toward Liselle. "She's okay. You're okay. Can you try to stand, honey?"

Honey. Liselle closed her eyes, righted her ankle, and smoothed her skirt. It could have been worse. She began trying to sit up, still clutching the four twenty-dollar bills.

"Xochitl," she said. "Here you go."

The guests stood around looking at one another. Xochitl looked unembarrassed as she took—and counted—the money. "Thank you," she said. "But are you . . ."

She took Xochitl's hand instead of her husband's, but she eyed him. "I'm okay. Party's not over yet."

t the beginning of October in 1994, Liselle had read in *City Paper* about a new hip-hop and R&B party at the club Fluid, just off South Street. She had misgivings, but told Selena about it.

Selena grinned. "It's gonna be *wet*."

"Ugh," said Liselle. "A bunch of wet *dicks*."

"Look," said Selena, "wouldn't it be nice to go be with some Black people being natural? And dance to some decent music? I'm bored of being stuck here." She gestured around to Liselle's bedroom, the Gil Scott-Heron and Grace Jones posters drooping from inadequate adhesive to cement block walls.

"Bored of being stuck here? Are you really?" said Liselle in what she thought was a sultry voice, leaning in. Selena broke away from their kiss.

"Yes," she said. "I am bored."

She was transformed, Liselle reflected. Those first few weeks, she had been hesitant, somewhat awed by Liselle's interest and confidence. Now she asked for things. Everyone went through this in college, but for most people the changes came after a few years, not a few months.

"Well, fine," said Liselle. "But there's going to be sweaty dudes trying to push up on you and I can't do anything about that."

Selena smirked. "Why would I need you to?"

"Also, you know they card. I mean, some of us are twenty-one, but . . ."

Selena, who'd had a fake ID since junior year of high school, rolled her eyes. "How is it I'm dating someone three years older than me who is such a *widdle baby?*"

Liselle kept up a constant stream of chatter on the journey: the dark walk to the Bryn Mawr train station, waiting at the rail stop, on the train to Thirtieth Street, at the el stop, the el ride, and walking from Market to South Street. She tried to play down the fact that she was nervous about holding her girlfriend's hand. It was chilly and she needed her hands in her pockets, she claimed. Nearly two hours after they started out, they got chicken steaks at Ishkabibble's. Liselle wound up tossing most of her sandwich; her stomach fluttered unpleasantly.

The party was on the second floor of a restaurant. At 10:00 p.m., only a few souls haunted the dance floor. A thin woman with a freakishly long neck and clad in flowing African fabrics appeared to be improvising an avant-garde routine while the DJ warmed up with seemingly endless Fela Kuti tracks. Men of different sizes and sensibilities stood around the floor, moving so slightly they almost weren't moving. There was a group of girls, a rare congress of hair weaves *and* naturals, investing a lot in seeming busy. Liselle and Selena tasted each other's drinks, declared them weak, and leaned on a table, nodding to the music. Then the DJ switched over to hip-hop; when "Juicy" by Biggie played, men started to circulate more assertively.

Feeling alone and on display, Liselle watched as a girl walked up to the DJ and whispered something in his ear. She walked away with an angry look on her face; she and her friends looked back at the DJ, laughing in that way girls laugh when they want you to hear them. Liselle studied the melting ice left by her drink; when she looked up she saw Selena headed over toward the DJ and saw what the DJ saw: short denim skirt and high ponytail, dreads spilling out. The prettiest girl there. The room abruptly filled with the clanging sounds of Wu-Tang. Selena liked hard music. She liked Jodeci ballads only because Jodeci seemed scary.

Liselle and Selena danced side by side, barely touching, in stark contrast with the straight white girls mounting faux lesbian burlesque. Then an unusually tall light-skinned guy got between them facing Selena, his back to Liselle. Before Liselle had a chance to experience her feelings about this, a wiry man with an encouraging smile was jumping around in front of Liselle. She remembered how at high school parties there had been a historical moment when boys stopped asking you to dance and instead just sidled up behind you. Back then she had tried to like it. In this moment, she was clear with herself: as sex it was gross; as sport, sublime. She matched her movements to the man in front of her; his smile widened. She caught sight of Selena's glistening face and smiled inwardly.

While Liselle danced with people sporadically, Selena entertained a steady stream of partners, occasionally pleading for rest. Liselle sipped another vodka and cranberry, told herself not to feel bad about not being chosen by boys. She had already won the prize. As her thoughts spun out, the room became crammed with people, a number of them white and willing to try to dance-off in the middle of the floor, regardless of skill level.

About an hour and a half passed with Selena mostly dancing and Liselle mostly leaning on a nearby table. She tried to stuff down a mounting sense of panic, to enjoy the music and "Black people being natural," but after a short bodybuilder type walked away, she leaned into Selena's ear.

"We have to get on the last train, unless you want to meet Verity."

Selena grinned. "Whose house do you think would be worse to turn up at? Yours or mine?" Then another male human, wearing sunglasses in the dark club, appeared and lunged at Selena's hand.

"I'm on a break," she said, smiling.

"What about you?" he said to Liselle.

"I'm okay."

He began to walk away, but then he backed up, leaning into their faces. "Tell me this. Why do bitches even come to the club?"

Suddenly there was someone with him, another man, with an apologetic look. "Excuse me, ladies. Don't mind my cousin. He just got out of jail and had one White Russian too many." He put his arm around the other's broad shoulders.

"Aw, fuck you, man," protested the first one. "Don't act like you never did time. And I don't ever drink anything white, not even milk!" He allowed himself to be steered away even as he continued to loudly defend his honor and decry the snobbishness of bitches.

Selena's resigned look pierced Liselle. She thought about the scene in *Zami* where Audre and Afrekete walk the streets of Harlem holding hands, while Black men smile, embracing them as sisters. The professor had said this was a fantasy sequence, the myth of the mythography.

Before any other bullshit could happen, Liselle grabbed Selena's hand and pulled her into a tight spot on the dance floor, using nearby white girls for cover. The DJ played a Tribe song, one of Selena and Liselle's favorites, and they swayed together, *Honey, check it out, you got me mesmerized with your black hair and fat-ass thighs* . . . First they faced each other, and then Selena turned around and Liselle brushed against the back of her so gently it almost hurt.

When the song changed again, they pushed out of the circle, ran down the stairs and into the throng of South Street, laughing as if they'd pulled off the final heist.

It was a long, cold journey back to campus. They held hands all the way.

L iselle ignored Winn's questioning look as she walked over to the small mounted black box piping music through the house and turned it off.

"Can I help you guys clean up?" asked Ron.

"Sure, Ron," she said over Winn's refusal noises. "That would be great." Winn had always treated Ron with an exaggerated deference (Liselle thought, to cover his actual deference). But she had a strong inkling that come what may, Ron sure as fuck wasn't going to prison. The least he could do was bring some plates into the kitchen.

"I will help too," said Gladys, but she stayed on the sitting room couch while Ron, Vanessa, and Ivelisse moved back toward the dining room table.

The "Dinner with Edge" mix had ended while she was fighting with Winn, and it was definitely time for everyone to go home, but the silence of the house made her feel naked.

"Don't mind me," she said sharply, feeling baffled stares as she knelt gingerly at the bottom of the stereo cabinet in the front room, where she still kept her all-time favorites in vinyl. She stood and placed a record on the turntable. Stevie Wonder's fake Spanish poured forth. It was the first song that Patrice, at three years old, had ever loved. He had adored the fake Spanish; had developed a language out of it. He used it to curse them when he was angry, jabbing his little finger in the air. He had called the song "Worry." "I want 'Worry,'" he would say.

Winn stood by the sideboard, still holding a tumbler, with the look of a confused baby. Liselle listened to the music and imagined herself dancing. Then she was dancing, doing the little crude step she had learned a long time ago at the lesson before salsa night at a Manhattan club. It was one of the two times that she, Winn, Sasha, and Luther had gone out in the evening. That night only she and Luther had danced with some success. Sasha had clawed furiously at her sleeves and Winn, it seemed, could not count to three.

The structure of the song was a map in her brain. It had been one of Verity's favorites, and Liselle had played it many times at Patrice's demand, but she never tired of it. Everybody's got a thing; some don't know how to handle it. Always reaching out in vain, just taking the things not worth having. Don't you worry 'bout a thing. She wondered if she'd get to know Patrice anew. *After my dad went to prison, it was just me and Mom against the world*, he'd say.

Ron, Ivelisse, and Vanessa had abandoned the cleaning and were back in the room. Gladys was up dancing solo, moving alone with dainty arrhythmic steps. Vanessa stabbed at the floor with her heels and glared. Liselle had learned somewhere that the severe look had come with the slaves; an African dance face. Ron, who was trying, Liselle thought, not to dance with Ivelisse, took Vanessa's hands, imitating her strong step. Liselle worried the record would skip. Liselle found herself dancing with Chris. He was, of course, smooth and fluid in the endeavor.

"Where did you learn to dance salsa?" she asked.

"I was literally born knowing," he said.

"Can I cut in?" said Winn, still clutching his cocktail glass. Liselle looked at him. Then she took the drink.

"Go ahead," she said, motioning him toward Chris, who laughed a high-pitched laugh and shook his head.

"You are excellent," he said.

Winn took the drink from her and put it next to the stereo. Then he took her hands in his. Though she tried to show him the steps, he resisted, proposing his own. And so they fumbled. The way he forced her to move revived the pain in her ankle.

"Soon," William McMichael had said, and Liselle thought she heard the doorbell underneath the music. But she didn't stop dancing. Then came the part of the song where it sounds like going around and round. Her ankle began to throb, but she couldn't abandon Winn while other people were dancing. When Vanessa let Ron go to dance with Ivelisse, he tried to take Gladys in hand. Even peripherally, Liselle could see her stiffen. "I don't dance," she said loudly over the music; she resumed dancing when Ron walked away. Ivelisse dipped Vanessa. Liza and Gary moved wildly (one could not say *together*), disregarding song style and rhythm. Occasionally Liselle could forgive white people for doing that, if they were not too shitty otherwise as humans. Just as she had this thought, Winn stepped lightly on her foot.

Someone was definitely at the door; Liselle heard banging under the music. A phrase popped into her mind: *being Black at the end of the world*. Just then she locked eyes with Vanessa, who tilted her head toward the front of the house and made a slight hand motion. *Just keep dancing*, she seemed to say as she stomped off.

The octave changed, signaling the beginning of the song's end.

These days when she played it, Liselle often tried to stop time, superstitiously starting it again before the silence or the next song. But now her ankle hurt and she was tired. *Don't worry, don't worry,* don't *worry!* Vanessa reappeared in the room, a woman at her side.

And there she was: Selena.

ACKNOWLEDGED

I want to thank Andrew Friedman for absolutely everything and Adebayo and Mkale for loving life as they do.

Thanks again to my agent, Ellen Levine, who has always been so steady, and the wonderful Martha Wydysh. Thanks to Jenna Johnson for seeing this through with passion and intelligence, and to the splendid production people, designers, and publicity people at Farrar, Straus and Giroux. Thank you, Lorna Simpson.

Some people contributed information or weighed in on some aspect of this novel. They include Samara Wiley; Evie Shockley, who politely listened to an early elevator pitch and (politely) said, "I'd like to read that," but I took it seriously; Alexis Pauline Gumbs; Camille Acker; and Akiba Solomon. Thanks also to the Claw and Sandra Lim for commiseration and strategy.

Thank you to my colleagues at Haverford College, especially in the English department.

Thanks to Rochelle and James, the AME thread, Linda Kim, and Suite 34.

This list is precise and book-specific. There is an absurdly long list of others who made me feel rooted and rooted for while working on this, and while surviving the past two years on earth. That list is a whole other book. I carry it in my head and in my heart.

A Note About the Author

Asali Solomon's first novel, *Disgruntled*, was named a best book of the year by the *San Francisco Chronicle* and *The Denver Post*. Her first book, *Get Down*, earned her a Rona Jaffe Foundation Writers' Award and the National Book Foundation's "5 Under 35" honor, and was a finalist for the Hurston/Wright Legacy Award. Her work has appeared in *O, The Oprah Magazine*, *Vibe*, *Essence*, *The Paris Review Daily*, *McSweeney's*, and several anthologies, and on NPR. Solomon teaches fiction writing and literature of the African diaspora at Haverford College. She was born and raised in Philadelphia, where she lives with her husband and two sons.